THE WRONG SET

THE WRONG SET

and other stories

by
ANGUS WILSON

LONDON
SECKER & WARBURG
1949

Martin Secker & Warburg Ltd.
7 John Street, Bloomsbury, London, W.C.1.

First published 1949

PRINTED IN GREAT BRITAIN
BY THE ALCUIN PRESS, WELWYN GARDEN CITY AND BOUND
BY KEY AND WHITING LTD., LONDON

To

BENTLEY AND IAN

in gratitude

"Mother's Sense of Fun" and "Crazy Crowd" were first published in *Horizon* and "Real-politik" in *The Listener*.

CONTENTS

CONTENTS

Fresh Air Fiend

IT had rained heavily the night before and many of the flowers in the herbaceous border lay flattened and crushed upon the ground. The top-heavy oriental poppies had fared worst; their hairy stalks were broken and twisted, and their pink and scarlet petals were scattered around like discarded material in a dress-maker's shop. But they were poor blowsy creatures anyway, thought Mrs. Searle, the vulgar and the ostenta-tious survive few blows. Nevertheless she chose sticks and bast from the large trug which she trailed behind her, and carefully tied the bent heads, cutting off the broken ones with the secateurs. It was at once one of the shames and one of the privileges of gardening, she thought, that one was put in this godlike position of judgment, deciding upon what should live and what should be cast into outer darkness, delivering moral judgments and analogies. It was only by a careful com-pensation, an act of retribution, such as preserving the poppies she had condemned, that she could avoid too great an arrogance. She fingered the velvety leaves of the agrostemma sensuously, there were so few flowers of exactly that shade of rich crimson, and how gloriously they lay against their silver foliage. There should be more of them next year—but less, she decided, of the scarlet lychnis, there was nothing more disappointing than a flower spike on which too few blooms appeared. Ragged, meagre and dowdy for all their bright colours, like the wife of the Warden of St. Jude's. How depress-ing that one still remembered that dispiriting little woman

sitting there talking in her slight North country accent,
and dressed in that absurd scarlet suit.

"Your signature on this petition, Mrs. Searle, would
be such a help. If we University women can give a lead.
. . . I mean we've all too easily decided that war is inevit-
able, it's only by thinking so that we make it, you know."
"Of course", she had found herself answering mockingly
"who can understand that better than I? You don't
remember the last war, but I do. Those hundreds of
Belgians, each without a right arm. Oh! it was terrible".
The ridiculous little woman had looked so puzzled that
she had been unable to resist embroidering. "Don't you
know Belgium then?" she had said. "Not a man there
to-day with a right arm, and very few with right eyes.
Those were all gouged out with hot irons before the
Kaiser himself. To make a Roman holiday, of course".
The woman had gone away offended. Silly little creature,
with all her petitions she had been most anxious to prove
her ardour in the war when it came, although of course
like everyone in Oxford she had been perfectly safe. How
they had all talked of the terrible raids, and how they had
all kept out of them. At least she had preserved her
integrity. "Thousands killed brutally in London last
night" she had said to the Master "and everyone of us
preserved intact. What a glorious mercy!" They thought
she was mad, and so she was, of course, judged by their
wretched middle class norm. "I hereby faithfully swear
once more" she said aloud "that I will make no compromise, and I utterly curse them from henceforth. May
no wife of any fellow in either of the major Universities
be fecund, nor may the illicit unions of research students
be blessed", and she added maliciously "May the stream
of sherry so foolishly imported by this present government be dried up, so that there may be no more 'little

sherry parties'." It was monstrous when things of importance—spirits for example—were in short demand—though what such jargon really meant one was at a loss to understand—that such frivolities as sherry parties should be indulged.

Suddenly she could hear that other voice inside her speaking slowly and distinctly, counting in the old, familiar fashion—two bottles of gin in the trunk in the attic, two in the garden shed, one in the bureau, she had the key to that, and then one in the bottom of her wardrobe with the shell mending box. The bureau one was a bit risky, Henry occasionally used that, but with the key in her possession . . . six bottles in all. I'll send Henry down with that girl to the pub for a drink before lunch and they'll be out walking this afternoon, she decided. It had seemed as though the girl's presence would make things difficult, Henry had obviously hoped so when he had invited her, but by retiring early and leaving them to talk it had been managed. . . .

The voice shut off and Mrs. Searle gave zealous attention to the flowers once more. The clumps of lupins were massed like an overpainted sunset—anchovy, orange and lemon against skyblue—only the very top of their spikes had been bent and hung like dripping candles. The crests of the delphiniums were broken too, and the petals lay around pale iceblue and dark blue like scattered boat race favours. Mrs. Searle shrank back as she surveyed the tall verbascums; their yellow flowers were covered in caterpillars, many of which had been drowned or smashed by the rain, their bodies now dried and blackening in the hot sun. "Miss Eccles, Miss Eccles" she called "are you good with caterpillars?"

A very tall young woman got up from a deck chair on the lawn and moved lopingly across to the flower bed;

the white linen trousers seemed to accentuate her lumbering gait and her ungainly height; her thin white face was cut sharply by the line of her hard, vermilion lipstick; her straight, green-gold hair was worn long at the neck. "I'll see what I can do, Mrs. Searle" she said, and began rapidly to pick off the insects. "But you *are* good with caterpillars" said Miranda Searle. "It's a gift, of course, like being good with children. I'm glad to say that I hold each in equal abhorrence. Don't you think the verbascum very beautiful? I do, but then it's natural I *should* like them. I share their great quality of spikiness". If you were covered with caterpillars, thought Elspeth Eccles, I wouldn't budge an inch to remove them, I should laugh like hell. She had always believed that absolute sincerity was the only basis for human relationships, and she felt convinced that a little truth telling would work wonders with Mrs. Searle's egotistical artificiality, but somehow she shrank from the experiment of telling her hostess what she really thought of her spikiness, there was no doubt that for all her futility and selfishness she was a little daunting. It was the difference of age, of course, and the unfair superiority of riches, but still she preferred to change the topic. "What are those red and blue flowers with the light foliage?" she asked. "Linum" replied Mrs. Searle. "You know—'Thou wilt not quench the burning flax, nor hurt the bruiséd reed', only that doesn't sound quite right". "It certainly seems a little meaningless" commented Elspeth. "Oh! I should hope so" said Mrs. Searle. "It's religious. You surely wouldn't wish a religious sentiment to have a meaning. It wouldn't be at all edifying. I doubt if it would even be proper". Elspeth smiled to herself in the conviction of her own private creed. "No, it's the phrase 'bruiséd reed' that I detest" said Mrs. Searle. "It reminds me too much of 'broken reed'. Have you ever been in the W.V.S.?" she went on. "Oh blessed generation! Well, *I* have. Henry made me join the Oxford W.V.S. during the war, he said it was my duty. A curious sort of duty, I did nothing but serve cups of sweet dishwater to men with bad teeth. But what I was thinking of was the way all the women talked in clichés—throughout the winter they described themselves as 'chilly mortals', and whenever anyone failed to do some particularly absurd task, as I frequently did, they called them 'broken reeds'. But I am keeping you from your work, Miss Eccles" she went on "and Henry will never forgive that. It must be wonderful for you both to have a common interest in so many vulgar people. Though perhaps in the case of the Shelley circle, as I believe it's called—it is Shelley you're working on?"— It was the seventh time in five days that she had asked the question, Elspeth noted—"as I say in the case of the Shelleys it is more their priggish refinement than their vulgarity that revolts me".

"Perhaps it's their basic honesty you dislike" said Elspeth. "Very likely" said Mrs. Searle "I hadn't realized that they were particularly honest. But if that were so, of course, I should certainly dislike it. How very nice it must be to know things, Miss Eccles, and go about hitting nails on the head like that. But seriously, you mustn't let me keep you from the Shelleys and their orgy of honesty". On Elspeth's assurance that she would like to remain with her, Mrs. Searle suggested that they should go together to gather gooseberries in the kitchen garden.

Elspeth watched her depart to collect a basin from the house. It was difficult, she thought, to believe that people had once spoken of her as the "incomparable Miranda". Of course the very use of such names suggested an affected gallantry for which the world no longer had time, but, apart from that, the almost Belsen-like emaciation of figure and features, the wild, staring eyes and the whispy hair that defied control hardly suggested a woman who had inspired poets and tempted young diplomats; a woman whose influence had reached beyond University society to the world of literary London, rivalling even Ottoline Morrell herself. A faint look of distressed beauty about the haggard eyes, an occasional turn of the head on that swanlike neck were all that remained to recall her famed beauty, and even these reminded one too much of the Lavery portraits. No, decidedly, she thought it was all too easily described by one of Mrs. Searle's own favourite words—"grotesque". Of the famous charm too, there were only rare flashes, and how like condescension it was when it came, as in some ornate fairy story of the 'nineties when the princess gives one glimpse of heaven to the poor poet as her coach passes by. That may have been how Rupert Brooke and Flecker liked things, but it wouldn't have done to-day. That crabbed irony and soured, ill natured malice, those carefully administered snubs to inferiors and juniors, could that have been the wit that had made her the friend of Firbank and Lytton Strachey? It seemed impossible that people could have tolerated such arrogance, have been content with such triviality. It was unfair, probably, to judge a galleon by a washed up wreck. There was no doubt that at some period Miranda Searle had strayed, was definitely *détraquée*. Even her old friends in Oxford had dropped her, finding the eccentricity, the egotism, the rudeness insupportable. But to Elspeth it seemed that such a decline could not be excused by personal grief, other mothers had had only sons killed in motor accidents and had lived again, other women had been confined to provincial lives and had kept their charity. It was monstrous that a man of the intellectual calibre of Henry Searle, a man whose work was so important should be chained to this living corpse. She had heard stories already of Mrs. Searle's secret drinking and had been told of some of the humiliating episodes in which she had involved her husband, but it was not until this visit to their Somerset cottage that she had realized how continuous, how slowly wearing his slavery must be. On the very first night she had heard from her bedroom a voice raised in obscenities, a maundering whine. She had guessed—how right she had been—that this was one of the famous drinking bouts. It had enabled her to see clearly why it was that Henry Searle was slowly withdrawing from University life, why the publication of the last volume of Peacock's letters was delayed from year to year, why the projected life of Mary Shelley remained a dream. It was her duty, she had decided then, to aid him in fighting the incubus, her duty to English letters, her return for all the help he had given to her own labours. But how difficult it was to help anyone so modest and retiring, anyone who had evaded life for so long. She had decided, at last, that it would be easier to start the other end, to put the issue fairly and squarely before Mrs. Searle herself. If there was any truth in the excuse of her defenders, if it was in fact the shock of her son's sudden death, then surely she could be made to see that the living could not be sacrificed to the dead in that way. And yet, and yet, one hesitated to speak, it was the last day of the visit and nothing had been said. "It's now or never, Elspeth Eccles" she said aloud.

"My dear, Miss Eccles" her hostess drawled. "How this cheers me! To hear you talk to yourself. I was just beginning to feel daunted. Here she is, I thought, the representative of the 'hungry generations'—straight-forward, ruled by good sense, with no time for anything but the essential—and they're going to 'tread me down'. How can I? I thought, with all my muddled thinking and my inhibitions—only the other day that new, young physics tutor was telling me about them—how can I resist them? It seemed almost inhuman! And then I hear you talking to yourself. It's all right, I breathe again. The chink in another's armour, the mote in our brother's eyes, how precious they are! what preservers of Christian charity!" "That doesn't sound a very well-adjusted view of life" said Elspeth, in what she hoped was a friendly and humorous voice.

"Doesn't it?" said Miranda. "So many people say that to me and I'm sure you're all quite right. Only the words don't seem to connect in my mind and I do think that's so important, in deciding whether to think a thing or not, I mean. If I don't connect the words, then I just don't have the thought. And 'adjusted' never connects with 'life' for me, only with 'shoulder strap'."

With her wide brimmed straw hat, flowing sleeved chiffon dress, and her constantly shaking long earrings, Mrs. Searle looked like a figure at the Theatrical Garden Party. Laying down the box of Army and Navy Stores cigarettes which was her constant companion, she began rapidly to pick the gooseberries from the thorny bushes.

"Put them all into that bowl will you" she said, a cigarette hanging from the corner of her mouth. "I want Mrs. Parry to make a fool so we shall need a good number of them."

"Why do you need more to make a fool?" asked Elspeth. "Because of the sieving," said Miranda shortly and contemptuously.

The two women picked on in silence for some minutes.

To Elspeth, it seemed, that her own contribution was immensely the smaller; it seemed impossible that with those absurd, flowing sleeves and the smoke from that perpetual cigarette Mrs. Searle could pick with such ease. Her own fingers were constantly being pricked by the thorns and the legs of her trousers got caught against the bushes.

"Poor Miss Eccles!" said Miranda. "You must stop at once or you'll ruin those lovely trousers. It was quite naughty of me to have suggested your doing such a horrid job in such beautiful clothes". Elspeth was crouching to pick some refractory fruit from a very low bush, but she stood up and remained quite still for a moment, then in a clear, deliberate voice, she said

"Now, you don't think they're beautiful clothes at all, Mrs. Searle. You probably think trousers on women are the height of ugliness, and in any case they cannot compare for elegance with your lovely dress. It's just that I'm clumsy and awkward in my movements, and you are graceful and easy. What makes you unable to say what you think of me?"

Mrs. Searle did not answer the question, instead she stared at the girl with rounded eyes, then throwing her cigarette on the ground she stamped it into the earth with her heel.

"Oh Miss Eccles" she cried "how lovely you look! Now I understand why Henry admires you so. You look so handsome, so noble when you are being stern, just like Mary Wollestoncraft or Dorothy Wordsworth or one of those other great women who inspire poets and philosophers".

"How can you say that, Mrs. Searle?" cried Elspeth "You who knew and inspired so many of our writers".

B

"Oh no!" said Miranda. "I never inspired anyone, I just kept them amused. I was far too busy enjoying life to *inspire* anyone".

"Then why can't you go on enjoying life now?" "Oh! Miss Eccles, how charming of you! I do believe you're paying me a compliment, you're being sincere with me and treating me as one of your own generation. But you forget that 'you cannot teach an old dog new tricks'. And now look what you've done, you've made me use an ugly, vulgar proverb". "I don't think it's a question of generations" said Elspeth "it's just a matter of preferring to have things straight instead of crooked. Anyway if people of my age are more straightforward it's only because we've grown up in a world of wars and economic misery where there's only time for essentials".

Mrs. Searle looked at her with amusement. "If it comes to essentials" she said "elegance and beauty seem to me far more essential than wars".

"Of course they are" said Elspeth "but they can't have any reality until we've straightened out the muddle and misery in the world".

"In the world?" echoed Miranda. "I should have thought ones own private miseries were enough".

"Poor Mrs. Searle" said Elspeth "it must have hit you very badly. Were you very fond of him? Did they break the news clumsily? Won't you tell me about it?" And she wondered as she said it whether she did not sound a little too much as though she were speaking to a child, but after all the woman was a child emotionally, a child that was badly in need of re-education.

Miranda stopped picking for a minute and straightened herself; when she looked at Elspeth, she was laughing.

"Oh my dear Miss Eccles! I do believe you're trying to get me to 'share'. And I never even guessed that you were a Grouper".

"I'm not a Grouper" said Elspeth. "I'm not even what you would call religious, that is I don't believe in God" she added lamely.

But Miranda Searle took no notice. "Oh what fun!" she cried. "Now you can tell me all about those house-parties and the dreadful things that people confess to. I've always wanted to hear about that. I remember when the Dean of St. Mary's shared once. He got up in public and said that he'd slept with his niece. It wasn't true, of course, because I know for a fact that he's impotent. But still it was rather sweet of him, because she's a terribly plain girl and it gave her a sexual cachet that brought her wild successes. After that I went through Oxford inventing the most wonderful things that I said people had shared with me until I was threatened with libel by the entire Theological Faculty."

"Oh, it's quite impossible" said Elspeth and in her agitation she overturned the bowl of gooseberries. She felt glad to hide her scarlet face and her tears of vexation in an agitated attempt to pick them up.

"Oh please, please" said Miranda. "It couldn't matter less". At that moment the tweed-clothed knickerbockered figure of Mr. Searle came down the path towards them. "Henry" called his wife. "Henry, you never told me Miss Eccles was a 'Grouper'. She was just going to share with me, and it must have been something very exciting because it made her upset the gooseberries. Take her down to the pub for a drink. That's just the place for a good man to man sharing. Perhaps you can get that barmaid to tell you what goes on in Hodge's field, or Mr. Ratcliffe might even confess about that poor goat.   Whatever you find out you must report to me at once".

Mr. Searle put down his glass of port, and drawing his handkerchief from the sleeve into which it was tucked, he carefully wiped his neatly trimmed grey moustache. With his well worn dinner jacket and his old patent leather pumps he looked far more like a retired military man or an impoverished country squire than a Professor of English Poetry, and so he would have wished it. The evening had been hot and the French windows had been left open; a cool night breeze had begun to invade the room. Now that Mrs. Searle had gone upstairs Elspeth felt able to put her little blue woollen coat round her shoulders. She had decided to wear an evening dress as a concession to her host's formality, and yet it was largely the presence of her hostess with her long brocade gown that had kept her to the decision after the first evening. She felt sad that this was the last of their talks together— talks which she enjoyed all the more for the elegance of the room and the glass of kümmel which he was careful to pour out for her each evening, though she felt that to admit to such sensual pleasure was in some sense a capitulation to Miranda's influence in the house. But once her hostess had retired, the sense of strain was gone and she could adopt a certain hedonism as of her own right. No doubt he would have to face the same sordid scene to-night, no doubt he would have to face such bouts on and off until that woman died. She had failed lamentably this morning to achieve anything. But, at least, their discussions together had freed him from the strain, had allowed him to relax. I shall try once more, she thought, to make him talk about it, to impress upon him that his work is too important to be shelved for someone else's selfishness, that he must assert himself. This time I must act more subtly, less directly.

"There seems no doubt" she said "that the Naples birth certificate is genuine. A child was born to Shelley by some one other than Mary, and that person could hardly have been Claire Clairemont, despite all Byron's ugly gossip. The question is who was the mother?"

"Yes" said Professor Searle. "It's a mystery which I don't suppose will be solved, like many others in Shelley's life. I sometimes doubt whether we have any right to solve them. Oh! don't think I'm denying the importance of the biographical element in literary appreciation. I know very well how much a full knowledge of a writer's life, yes, I suppose even of his unconscious life, adds to the interpretation of his work; particularly, of course, with any writers so fundamentally subjective as the Romantics. But I'm more and more disinclined to expose skeletons that have been so carefully buried. I suppose it's a reticence that comes with old age" he added.

"I doubt if it's a defensible standpoint" said Elspeth. "Think of the importance of Mary Shelley's relations with Hogg and with Peacock, what a lot they explain of Shelley's own amoral standpoint towards married fidelity. Or again, how much of Leigh Hunt's instability and failure can be put down to the drain of his wife's secret drinking".

"Yes, I suppose so" said Professor Searle. "But when one appreciates a man's work deeply, it means in the long run respecting him and respecting his wishes. You see it isn't only the revealing of facts that have been carefully hidden, it's our interpretation that may be so vitally wrong, that would hurt the dead so. We blame Mary for her infidelity and Mrs. Hunt for her insobriety, but who knows if that is not exactly the thing that Shelley and Hunt would most have hated? Who knows if they did not hold themselves responsible?"

Elspeth spoke quite abruptly. "Do you hold yourself responsible for *your* wife's drinking?" she asked.

Professor Searle drained his glass of port slowly, then he said "I've been afraid that this would happen. I think you have made a mistake in asking such a question. Oh! I know you will say I am afraid of the truth, but I still think there are things that are better left unsaid. But now that you have asked me I must answer—yes, in a large degree, yes".

"How? how?" asked Elspeth impatiently.

"My wife was a very beautiful woman and a very brilliant one. Not the brilliance that belongs to the world of scholars, the narrow and often pretentious world of Universities, but to a wider society of people who act as well as think. Don't imagine that I do not fully recognize the defects of this wider world—it is an arrogant world, placing far too great a value upon what it vaguely calls 'experience', too often resorting to action to conceal its poor and shoddy thinking; as a young scholar married to a woman of this world its faults were all too apparent to me. Nevertheless, however I may have been a fish out of water there, it was her world and because I was afraid of it, because I did not shine there, I cut her off from it, and in so doing I embittered her, twisted her character. There were other factors, of course, the shock of our boy's death did not help, and then there were other things" he added hurriedly "things perhaps more important".

"Well, I think that's all fudge" said Elspeth. "You have something important to give and you've allowed her selfish misery to suck your vitality until now it is doubtful whether you will ever write any more".

"I am going to do the unforgivable" said Prof. Searle. "I am going to tell you that you are still very young. I doubt if my wife's tragedy has prevented me from continuing to write, though I *could* excuse my laziness in that way. What takes place between my wife and me has occurred so often now, the pattern is so stereotyped, that, awful though it may be, my mind, yes, and my feelings have become hardened to the routine. To you, even though it is only guessed at, or perhaps for that very reason, it will seem far more awful than it can ever again seem to me. That is why, although I had hoped that your visit might help the situation, I soon realized that pleasant as it has been and I shall always remember our discussions, the presence of a third person, the possibility that you might be a spectator was weighing upon me heavily". He lit a cigarette and sat back in silence. Why did I say that? he thought, I ought first to have crossed my fingers. So far we have avoided any scene in the presence of this girl, but by mentioning the possibility I was tempting Providence. This evening too, when the danger is almost over, and yet so near, for Miranda had clearly already been drinking when dinner was served, and these scenes come about so suddenly.

"Well, my dear" he said "I think we had better retire. Don't worry, perhaps I shall finish the Peacock letters this long vacation. Who knows? I've got plenty of notes and plenty of time. And, please, whatever I may have said, remember that your visit has been a most delightful event in my life".

But he had made his decision too late. In the doorway stood Miranda Searle, swaying slightly, her face flushed, her hand clutching the door lintel in an effort to steady herself.

"Still sharing?" she asked in a thick voice, then she added with a coarse familiarity. "You'll have to stop bloody soon or we'll never get to sleep". Her husband got up from his chair. "We're just coming" he said quietly. Miranda Searle leant against the doorway and laughed; points of light seemed to be dancing in her eyes as malice gleamed forth. "Darling" she drawled in her huskiest tones "the 'we' sounds faintly improper, or are we to carry the sharing principle to the point of bed?"

Elspeth hoisted her great height from the chair and stood awkwardly regarding her hostess for a second. "That's a very cheap and disgusting remark" she said. Henry Searle seemed to have lost all life, he bent down and touched a crack in his patent leather slippers. But the malicious gleam in Miranda's eyes faded, leaving them cold and hard. "Washing dirty linen in public is disgusting" she said, and as she spoke her mouth seemed to slip sideways. "Not that's there much to share. You're welcome to it all. He's no great cop, you know". She managed by the force of her voice to make the slang expression sound like an obscenity. "I pumped one kid out of him, but it finished him as a man".

Professor Searle seemed to come alive again, his hand went out in protest; but his resurrection was too slow, before he could cross the room Elspeth had sprung from her chair. Towering over the other woman she slapped her deliberately across the face, then putting her hands on her shoulders she began to shake her.

"You ought to be put away" she said. "Put away where you can do no more harm".

Miranda Searle lurched to get free of the girl's grasp, her long bony hands came up to tear at the girl's arms, but in moving she caught her heel in the rose brocade skirt and slipped ridiculously to the ground. The loss of dignity seemed to remove all her fury, she sat in a limp heap, the tears streaming from her eyes. "If they'd left me my boy, he wouldn't have let this happen to me", she went on repeating. Her husband helped her to her feet and, taking her by the elbow, he led her from the room. Elspeth could hear her voice moaning in the corridor. "Why did they take him away? What have I done to be treated in this way?" and the Professor's voice soothing, pacifying, reassuring.

It was many weeks later when Elspeth returned to Oxford. She spent the first evening of term with Kenneth Orme, the Steffansson Reader in Old Norse, also an ex-pupil of Professor Searle. To him she felt able to disclose the whole story of that fateful evening.

". . . . I didn't wait to see either of them the next morning" she ended. "I just packed my bag and stole out. I do not wish ever to see her again, and he, I felt, would have been embarrassed. It may be even that I have had to sacrifice his friendship in order to help". Elspeth hoped that her voice sounded calm, that Kenneth could not guess what this conclusion meant to her. "All the same whatever the cost I think it did some good. Drunk as she was I think she realized that there were some people with whom she could not play tricks, who were quite prepared to give her what she deserved. At any rate, it let a breath of fresh air into a very fetid atmosphere".

Kenneth Orme looked at her with curiosity. "Breaths of air can be rather dangerous" he said. "People catch chills from them, you know, and sometimes they are fatal chills".

"Oh, no fear of that with Miranda Searle" said Elspeth. "I wish there was, but she's far too tough".

"I wasn't thinking of Mrs. Searle" replied Kenneth. "I was thinking of the Professor. He's not returning this term, you know. He's had a complete breakdown."

Union Reunion

THEY could hardly keep their gaze on the low, one storeyed house as they came up the long, straight drive, so did the sunlight reflected from the glaring white walls hurt and crack their eyeballs. Down the staring white façade ran the creepers in streams of blood—splashes of purple and crimson bougainvillea pouring into vermilion pools of cannas in the flower beds below, the whole massed red merging into the tiny scarlet drops of Barbiton daisies and salvia that bordered the garden in trim ranks. The eyes of the visitors sought relief to the left of the verandah where the house came to an abrupt end, revealing the boundless panorama of the Umgeni valley beyond. The brown and green stretches of the plain lay so flat and seemed so near in the shimmering air that Laura felt as though she could have stretched out her hand to stroke the smooth levels far, far out into the white heat mists of the horizon, could have dabbled her fingers in the tiny streamer-like band of the great river as it curved and wound across the middle distance, and imitating Gulliver, could have removed with a simple gesture the clusters of corrugated iron huts with which Coolie poverty had marred the landscape. Here it lay—the background of her girlhood to which she had returned after twenty years and over so many thousands of miles.

For a moment she paused and stared into the distance. Nothing seemed to have changed since her childhood, and now it was as though its sleeping beauty had been awakened by the kiss of her sudden return. Thoughts and feelings which had lain dormant since she had left South Africa as a girl of twenty came pouring into her mind. Fragments of the scene had been with her, of course, throughout the years, distortedly as the background of her dreams or like flotsam attracted to the surface for a moment by some chance smell or sound in a London street, but always evasive, sinking back into the subconscious before she could see clearly. Now at last there was no puzzle; the blur of intervening years was gone and she saw it once more with the eyes of her youth.

But it was not with the Umgeni valley that she had to deal, it was with the family group drawn up to meet her. She could not indulge in the slow, soothing nostalgia of unchanged nature, must face the disturbing conflict of changed humanity. The harsh visual discord of the façade of the house seemed repeated upon the verandah with the men in their bright duck suits standing uneasily at the back and the women in their violently coloured linen and silk dresses seated in deck chairs in the foreground.

How enormous her sisters-in-law had grown, Laura reflected, but then it was easy to understand in this hot climate where they ate so much and moved so little; it was the price one had to pay for plentiful food and cheap motor-cars. Certainly the new short dresses with their low waists and shapeless bodices were not an advantage to stout women and made them look so many brightly painted barrels. She had been so angry at detecting superiority in Harry's manner towards her family on their arrival, but with all his faults she had married a man who appreciated smartness and, really, there was no other word for her sisters-in-law but blowsy. Flo, in particular, who had been such a fine, dark haired girl, almost Spanish looking people had said, seemed to have cheapened herself dreadfully. Harry had said she looked as though she kept a knocking shop and although, of course, it was a most unfair remark, one couldn't help laughing. Laura tried for a moment to visualize Flo at one of her bridge-parties in Kensington or Worthing—what *would* Lady Amplefield have said? The badly hennaed hair, the over-rouged cheeks and the magenta frock with its spray of gold flowers—could it be?—Yes, it actually was made of velvet, and in this heat; but it was wrong to make fun of Flo like that, for in spite of all that mischief makers might say, the doctor had told her that Flo had been very kind to her little David at the end. It was terrible to think of her son dying out here so far away from her and she tried never to dwell on it, but she must always be thankful to Flo for what she had done. That must be Flo's girl, Ursula, she decided, who was winding up the gramophone. How everyone seemed to like that "What'll I do?" But then waltz tunes were always pretty. She wondered whether her nieces had as many boys as she had had at their age. Of course it would all be different now, but though she had grown to accept the more formal standards demanded of young people in "the old country" she remembered with pleasure the free and easy life she had led as a girl, and that was in 1900 so what would it be like in this post-war world of 1924? Of course such ways wouldn't do in England, she quite saw that; but it had been a happy childhood. Here was Minnie coming to meet them. So she still took the lead in the family, and Flo and Edie probably still resented it; well more fools they for putting up with it. Minnie, at least, had kept some trace of her looks, with her corn-coloured hair and baby blue eyes, her skin too was still as delicate as ever, but she'd let her figure go. What a lot of one's

life was wasted in unnecessary jealousies, Laura thought,
as she watched her youngest sister-in-law approaching.
She could remember so well the countless picnics and
dances that had been spoilt for her through envy of
Minnie's tiny hands and feet and now such features were
not even particularly admired, and on poor Minnie's
mountainous body they looked positively grotesque.
She watched the enormous figure in powder blue muslin
teetering towards them on high-heeled white shoes, the
pink and white angel's face, with its pouts and dimples
and halo of golden hair, smiling and grimacing above the
swaying balloon-like body and she was filled with the
first revulsion she had felt that day. If only it had not
been Minnie with whom she had to make first contact.
She could not overcome her distrust and dislike of her
youngest sister-in-law. Her other sisters-in-law kissed
her and squeezed her arm and gave her confidences and
she did not shrink back, but with Minnie it always seemed
so false. Of course they had all felt that Minnie had
tricked Bert into the marriage and Bert had been her
favourite brother, but then it was all so long ago now and
Bert was dead. She really must try to forget these things,
being away so long had kept them fresh in her mind.
Queen Anne's dead, she said to herself with a grimace,
but she knew that she would never really forgive Flo and
Edie if they had forgotten that Minnie was an intruder
into the family. The clipped, pettish voice and the childish lisp had not disappeared anyway, she reflected, as her
sister-in-law's greeting became audible. Surely Harry
would not be fascinated with Minnie's baby talk now
that it came out of an elephant, as he had been in 1913
when Bert had brought his slim, attractive bride to London for their honeymoon.

Minnie at any rate was determined that her smart

English brother-in-law should remember their earlier flirtation. "But you're not changed at all, Harry" she said "not one tiny bit. Is he still as wicked as ever, Laura? But you needn't tell me, I can see he is. Well, you mustn't think you're going to play any of your tricks with the Durban girls of to-day. They're up to everything, they're not little schoolgirls like I was when I listened to all your stories. But still it was rather nice not knowing any better" she added, looking at Laura to see the effect of her words. "You've no right to have such an attractive husband, Laura, and if you have you should keep him under control. Laura hasn't changed either" she continued less confidently "but then we knew she'd be the same dear old Laura as ever" and she pressed her sister-in-law's arm. The family seized upon the formula eagerly.

Although Stanley and the other sisters-in-law had already seen Laura and Harry at the docks, this was the first family celebration of their visit. They had been awaiting this moment with nervous expectancy, there seemed to be so little in common except memories and yet it was not as if they could move immediately into the world of the past. After all they were not old people like Aunt Liz for whom past and present were irrevocably confused in a haze of sweet satisfaction. The contemplation of the past years still gave an immediate answer to them, the sum of what lay behind still added up to the mood of to-day, the business deal of to-morrow, the trip to the Cape next month. Unconsciously they had hoped that all difficulties would vanish in the mists of sentiment. It would give Aunt Liz such pleasure to hold a family reunion at her home, one was not eighty-eight every day; and then there was dear old Laura, she had had so many knocks, losing little David like that and if all the stories were true leading a dog's life with old Harry, having to

put up with other women and his gambling and extravagance, she deserved a break if anyone did, always so
proud and never letting on about her troubles, it would
do her good to feel the family were gathered round her.
So Stanley, the only living brother, reasoned and the
women fell in with the plan, partly from sentiment and
partly from curiosity, but chiefly as an exercise of their
matriarchal power. It was they who had declared war,
and now they would arrange a truce. If the meeting
provided nothing else, it would be an opportunity for
acquiring ammunition for the future—first-hand ob-
servation and scandal to replenish the decreasing stock of
hearsay.

The actual meeting, however, had not gone smoothly,
there were too many suspicions and jealousies to allow
conversation to flow freely, so that they had awaited
Laura's arrival to set the wheels in motion. Yet as soon
as they had seen her coming up the drive they had
realized that she too was a stranger, and something worse
than a stranger, an alien. Whatever their dissensions and
hatreds, and these still remained, they were South
Africans not only by birth but by life and habit, a feeling
of unity was sensed among them. Though Edie frowned
and turned aside when Flo whispered to her "She's still
very much the Duchess", Flo had hit upon the general
sentiment. Let Laura and Harry think them Colonials,
under the weight of that judgment they were at once
proud and ill at ease. Their childhood in common with
Laura was overshadowed by their memories of her as
they had seen her in London on their trips "home". Time
was needed before the community of the past, the ties of
kinship could be revived and Minnie had provided the
magic phrase to cover those first uneasy minutes when a
heightened awareness of what they were to-day seemed

to banish all hope of recapturing the sense of what they once had been. "The same dear old Laura as ever", the words bridged the gap between past and present. For the first few moments they all kept repeating it, and the fact that they none of them believed it seemed of no importance.

Rapidly the uneasiness and friction vanished as the drinks were handed round by the umfaan in his white cotton vest and shorts with their red edgings. The conflicting emotions of strangeness and of too great intimacy dissolved into the badinage and trivialities of the conventional middle class party.

The men stood in a group at the back of the verandah, helping themselves liberally to whiskies and sodas. Stanley with his pink, smooth, podgy face, his white trousers stretched like a drum over his swollen belly and fleshy rump, the two top fly buttons undone where the waistband would not meet, acted the genial host. Edie's two boys sprawled in deck chairs, bronzed, with a hidden and nervous virility, but with so great an external passivity that they appeared a neutral breed beside the aggressive self certainty of Harry's English raffishness as he chaffed his brother-in-law, patronized his nephews and laid down the law in consciousness of a superior sophistication. They were soon engaged in a series of arguments about sports and politics amid loud, boisterous laughter at jokes which came near to insults, their voices rising now and again in dogmatic assertions which trembled on the edge of loss of temper.

"My dear old pot-bellied, fat-headed friend" Harry was saying in answer to a poker story of Stanley's "if you care to raise the game on a busted flush you bloody well deserve to lose. You should give up poker, old boy, and take to tiddleywinks. Tiddleywinks would be your uncle's

C

strong suit," he added, turning to one of the boys. A moment later and they were involved in an argument upon a point of fact each asserting the superiority of his memory with a clamour that would have done credit to the Greens and Blues.

"No, no, Harry, you've got it wrong" Stanley asserted. "Maclaren never made a century during the whole of that tour. You're thinking of that famous innings of Lord Hawke's".

"Well since both Archie Maclaren and Martin Hawke are extremely old pals of mine I suppose I might be allowed to know something about it".

"You mustn't scare us with big names" said Stanley "we're only poor Colonials you know, Harry" and he winked at his nephews. But Harry knew when to take a joke against himself, in a moment he was expansive Britannia putting out a hand to pat the prize pupil on the head.

"Good God, Stanley, I don't know what we'd have done without you in '16, colonials or not" he said, his shoulders squared and his eyes staring straight ahead. "You put up a damned fine fight at Delville Wood. Don't think you aren't appreciated at home. Why they tell me the South Africans have put on the best show of the whole lot at Wembley. They're keeping it on next year, so you'll all have to come back with us, if they can find room for old Stanley in Piccadilly with all the traffic" he added laughing.

It was the Union's turn to be handsome now. "I'm afraid our racing's going to be small beer to you, Harry" said Stanley "but you must let me make you a member while you're here. I've bought one or two horses myself lately and I'd like to have your opinion on them".

"Glad to give it, old boy. As a matter of fact I was

talking to a pal of mine connected with the Manton stables just before we left and he asked me to keep my eyes skinned while I was over here. Said he'd heard you'd got one or two promising two year olds."

It was a proud moment and they all felt happy as they thought of praise from such a quarter. Emboldened by the conversation, Edie's younger boy ventured a question.

"What do you think of our Natal boys' rugger, Uncle Harry?" he inquired.

But Harry felt he had conceded enough. "Too busy studying the form of the Thirsty Tiddlers" he replied.

"Perhaps you don't know much about South African rugger" said the boy angrily. "I think. . . ."

"Don't laddie, don't" interrupted his uncle "it can be a very painful process if you haven't the requisite grey matter".

They were soon united again as the conversation turned to politics, for there was no Nationalist nonsense about Natal, everyone believed in Smuts and the S.A.P., everyone stood by the old country, yet what was the meaning of all this Labour and strikes, were the people at home turning Bolshie?

"Don't you worry about that" Harry answered them "It's just a crowd of agitators, like this Indian Saklatavala. He's a nasty piece of work—"

"That's our trouble" said Stanley "the Indians. We ought never to have allowed them to stay when their indentures were up. It was all due to master bloody Gandhi. We pretty near tarred and feathered him, you know, Harry, and we'd have slung him in the Bay as sure as life if old Sir Joseph hadn't stopped us. More's the pity. The trouble is it makes the native boys so difficult to handle. *They* have to be indoors at curfew and the coolies don't. You can't blame the Kaffirs for not liking it, but it's making them cheeky. You can't get a decent houseboy now, what with the missions and one thing and another".

"I'm sorry Stanley should choose to speak against the Mission boys" said Edie, her little bloodless lips compressed together in her sharp, yellowed and lined face.

"Take no notice of anything Stanley says, he just likes to hear himself talk. I know, I'm married to him" Flo drawled in her slow South African whine.

But the common topic of the natives had broken down the barrier between the two sexes, overshadowing the fascinations of sport and gambling for the men, of clothes and operations for the women. Only Laura and Harry remained unaffected, attempting to maintain the former flow of chatter. But Harry's jokes and Laura's oblique movements towards that other field of feminine interest— domestic service—were not proof against the intensity of emotions that welled up in the others. Pride and courage were high as they thought of all that had been achieved by the whites; yet, for a moment the anxieties and fears that were buried so deep shot through them with cruel sharpness as they thought of their small numbers and the thread by which their security hung. It was but a faint glimmer of their historical position that came to them, but, faint as it was, it was enough to outshine the selfishness of their everyday materialism. They sensed the brutal nature of their power, yet realized that if it was for a moment relaxed the answer would be swift and yet more brutal. The thought of the violence and the force upon which their lives rested excited them all, helping the gin and the whisky to thaw the gentility and pretension which ordinarily froze them, allowing the common crudity of their minds and feelings to flow and mingle.

To the women, in particular, this sense of danger, of brutal, even sexual violence was most strongly appealing and the nature of their answer to it least ashamed.

"I wonder you don't worry about your sister" said Flo to Edie. "I hear she's over fifty miles from the nearest white station, and I suppose her husband has to be away an awful lot".

"My sister's in God's hands and her own" said Edie grimly. "She doesn't fear for herself, that's why she's so respected. Norman says the natives are more afraid of her than they are of him".

"Well I should be terrified if my man wasn't there" drawled Flo "you hear of such dreadful cases in Zululand these days. It's always these educated boys, of course. An old school friend wrote me that she sleeps with a revolver under the pillow".

"That's because people have spoilt the natives" said Minnie. "We had over fifty boys on our farm in the old days and my father never had any trouble with them. If he had a boy who seemed cheeky, he gave him a taste of the sjambok. My brother does just the same now and *he* never has any trouble."

Even Aunt Liz's scattered memory was disturbed into some sort of equilibrium by the excitement of the topic.

"The sjambok isn't always enough" she croaked. "I shall never forget that boy we had called Whiskers, he was a real skellum. Your cousin was only a girl at the time, a skinny little thing. She was for ever complaining of faces looking in at her window, so your uncle and I waited outside all one night. Not that I was much size to deal with a man, but my blood was up and I'd have given him something to remember me by. It wasn't until early morning that he came creeping through the bushes by the back verandah. He must have seen us, I think, for he suddenly bolted, but your uncle didn't hesitate, he shot him through the foot. Oh, there's no doubt God watched over us in those days".

"And He does now, Auntie" said Edie piously.

The others, who had put off their nonconformity with their childhood, became embarrassed by the religious turn of the talk. Nevertheless they were proud as they looked at Aunt Liz, so frail and bent and shrivelled, what fine brave people they had been; those old pioneers! Really one felt ashamed to be so impatient with the old girl, even if she did forget who one was, and whine and complain so; they wouldn't see her like again, it was a dying breed. Laura, too, felt drawn back to the community of her family as she remembered the early days when Aunt Liz and Mother had come out from England, they had been windbound for six weeks or was it six days? anyway, for a very long time and eventually they had landed from the boat in baskets, fancy that, in baskets. There was no doubt that she came from a tough, pioneering stock who could hold their heads high. She looked proudly across at Harry as she turned to Aunt Liz.

"You certainly had hard times, Auntie" she said, smiling at the old lady, who had so far failed to recognize her. "Why I remember so well when the Zulus were coming south, though I was only five. Father was all ready to shoot us children if they should get as near as Maritzburg. Those were terrible days".

"If the Kaffirs attacked 'The Maples'" thought Minnie "I should have no man to defend me. Flo has Stanley and Laura has Harry, and Edie has her boys. I have no man. No woman was made to be petted and cared for more than me and yet I have no one. My hair is a lovely corn colour and my figure is beautiful; Mother always saw to it that I held myself well. I have to smile at the way they run round me. Even these raw Colonial boys see that I am a grand lady. It might be an English General or a foreign count. 'How can so small a hand be so lovely?' I trace figures in the sand with the tip of my cream lace parasol, but I do not look up. I am playing with him as Woman must. 'Why is she so mysterious, so enigmatic?' He has snatched a kiss and I am in my white muslin ball dress 'midst the scent of the geraniums, just a crazy girl after her first dance. No, perhaps more interesting than that, a woman of the world, lovely, with her white satin night dress clinging loosely about her limbs. 'You should not have come to my room. You may kiss my hand and then you must go.' Nothing nasty, no horrid contact, just a long flirtation, Woman's eternal spell cast over Man. I used to have such beautiful attachments, such wonderful affaires, only men always spoilt it, wanting to rush into bed, treating one so brutally, never content to worship at arm's length. And now there is not even that, no one even wanting my body now as Bert did, and Harry too, for all that Laura looks so proud. Now I am fat and shapeless and Harry hasn't noticed me, but I have not altered, I am still there smiling with my round blue eyes, kitten's eyes you used to call them, Harry. I should like to talk to him in our old baby language, to say 'Oo's naughty, Hawy, Minnie won't love 'oo if 'oo's so cruel'. They would all laugh at me. I shall scream and scream until he takes notice of me, he can't just let me scream. Dr. Gladstone did. I lay on the bed in my pink *crêpe de chine* and kicked and screamed. He said I disgusted him, that I looked like a pink jellyfish. Why am I unhappy? It ought to be so lovely for me, I was born for beauty and happiness. I can't bear it, I can't bear it. I won't face it. Come along Minnie, you're exaggerating, it's true you're not a girl any longer, but you're a woman of experience. Harry has made no sign yet because of Laura, but he will. 'You're grown up, Minnie, you're not my Baby any longer, but you're something much more, something that a mere man can only stand before in humble silence'. How kind and thoughtful Edie is, for all her narrow religion, she has put me next to Harry at dinner, it is now he will whisper to me under cover of the conversation."

The long dining table was so richly decked that hardly a trace of the white tablecloth could be seen beneath the array of polished silver, the napkins folded like rosebuds, and the scarlet and cream poinsettias twining their way among the cutlery. The old lady, though nominally hostess, had soon lost any real understanding of what was taking place. Stanley however had felt that a woman's hand was needed for so festive an occasion, so Flo had indulged to the full her taste for colour and decoration. The young people sat at a side table which was embellished with china models of Bonzo and Felix the cat. Stanley himself had seen to the menu and had ordered a massacre in the poultry yard that would have challenged Herod—a goose, a turkey, two ducks and two fowls had all shed their blood that Laura might feel welcome and Aunt Liz's eighty-eighth birthday not pass unhonoured. Edie presided over the vegetables, doling great heaps indiscriminately upon each plate—pumpkin, boiled rice, sweet potato, English potato, mealie cobs and peas and over all a thick brown gravy. If there were any protests she would put them aside with one of her dry little chapel jokes. "Nonsense, the Inner Man must be fed" she would say, or "You can't help your neighbour on an empty stomach". Laura at first felt a little shy at such profusion, remembering the toast Melba and vol au vent of Lady

Amplefield's luncheons in Hans Crescent, but the effect of three dry martinis and her childhood memories soon brought back the appetite of her youth. Aunt Liz ate greedily from her wheel chair, picking the wishbones in her fingers, and then dozed off before the second course. Everyone was anxious to know what Harry thought of the South African hock, and was relieved when he passed it as capital, though perhaps a shade sweet. Wait, they cried, till he tasted the Van Der Hum after the meal, then he would see what the Union could do. Apple pies, peach and apricot tarts, bright pink stewed guavas, bowls of pulpy salad made from pawpaw and granadilla followed, all covered with cream. Not until the fruit was on the table however did the clash of colour reach its highest note. In one bowl were the lichees with strange coral-like skins, and next to them the round granadillas, their wine-coloured shells cracked and dented like broken pingpong balls. In a third bowl were heaped the tawny mangoes flecked with black and smelling of the sugar refineries. In the centre of the table stood a cluster of pineapples, their tawny squares contrasting with the dozens of oranges of all sizes that surrounded them, from the tiny nartjies, through tangerines and green mandarins to the great navel oranges with their umbilical tops. For the discriminating palate there was savoury salad of avocado pear with its oily texture and its taste of dressed crab. But few palates were so discriminating as this and the avocado pear was eaten up in the mechanical round in which everything else was consumed, a deliberate locust-like advance that finally left the table a battlefield of picked bones, broken shells, dry skins and seeds.

The physical effects of such consumption of food and drink became increasingly marked as the meal progressed. Stanley's veins seemed to stand out in his temples, his neck seemed to swell and his brow to be bathed in sweat. Flo's high make-up became confused with an artificial and purple flush. Edie's face was suffused with a greasiness that seemed somehow to derive more from an inner piety than from the fatty liquids that clung to her faint black moustache. Laura's corsets were giving her trouble, whilst Minnie's flirtatious footplay with Harry was somewhat marred by an occasional hiccough. Indeed the belching and breaking of wind that soon began to visit the adults like a Mosaic plague was the occasion of much giggling and laughter at the side table. Aunt Liz awoke from her doze for one minute to a violent bout of flatulence.

"Did you hear that?" sniggered Edie's young son, and his elder brother whispered loudly "I think it was an Old Tin Lizzie backfiring".

It was not long before Stanley was caught up in the tide of coarseness that flowed from the juvenile table. With his bonhomie and his almost simple outlook he was always a favourite with the children. "Keep the seat warm for me" he called to his nephew as the latter departed for "where you can't go for me".

"Oh! Pop" shouted his daughter "don't you go to the loo, or you'll get stuck again" and they all went into peals of laughter at the famous family joke.

"I don't think even a crane would move you this time, darling" said his wife "you've got so broad in the beam".

By a coincidence Harry's voice was heard in man of the world explanation to Minnie—

"My dear girl, it's as broad as it's long". Even Edie had to join in the laugh and Stanley said with mock annoyance.

"You leave my behind out of your pow-wows".

"Oh, for God's sake" said Harry "keep your filthy

mind to yourself" and Minnie smiled sophisticated agreement, but they were in the minority. The heat of the room and the working of the digestive juices had completed the dissipation of self-consciousness begun by drink and family sentiment. Childhood was being recaptured in all its crudity.

A moment later Harry, anxious to accommodate himself to the company, attempted a hackneyed smoking-room story, but this was too great a sophistication, and, indeed, in its allusion to sex almost shocked Edie back into prudish gentility. Laura it was who saved the situation, taking up a chocolate, she smiled at her sister-in-law, "You'd better look at your bottom, Edie, mine's got paper stuck to it". Dear old Laura, she was one of the best, really, and "What price the Duchess?" whispered Flo.

Stanley picked up his glass and in a mock bow to his sister "Here's to you, Laura, your face my bottom". "You wretch" laughed his sister "I'd put you over my knee if I had half a chance".

After this sally of Stanley's, Edie's "Bottoms up" said with a giggle sounded a little feeble, but, still, coming from Aunt Edie! . . .

"Chase me, Charlie, chase me, Charlie, I've lost the leg of my drawers" hummed Flo. This was more like it, no silly airs and fancies, just like that funny picture in the album at home "A rare, old rickety rackety crew". There was nothing like a joke to make you feel young again and no one like Stanley to provide the joke, a real comical kid, think how he dressed up in the old girl's petticoats that night and kept them all in fits, pretending to get spooney. There he was now, though, winking and giggling at her, he'd probably want it before they got home. That was the trouble with him when he got tight,

always wanting it. Why can't they have a good time
without that? But it wasn't only the men who were the
cause, whatever women said. The women were half to
blame by fussing about it so. Look at Minnie, never so
happy as when she was leading them on and then going
all my lady and refusing them what they wanted, silly
cow. It wasn't as if there was anything to it, though she
liked a bit of fun herself occasionally, and if men wanted
it bad then it was nice to give it to them, like those poor
kids they sent out as Tommies in the War. But when it
was all over the best you got was to feel sleepy, now a
good party like this and having what you wanted that was
the way to live your life. That was one blessing in being
married to Stanley, he knew how to make money and he
knew how to spend it, not frittering it away with a lot of
splash, but having the comforts you wanted and putting
by for *anno Domini*. All the show Laura and Harry put
on, and Minnie too—uncrowned Queen of Durban that
English piano player had called her and how she lapped
it up. Well Stanley could buy them up any day that was
one satisfaction, and heaven knows what would happen
when they got old, come cap in hand to her probably,
and of course she'd fork out, for when all's said and done
blood's blood, but rather them than her. Comfort in old
age and the girls well provided for, that was what Stanley
and she had secured. It wouldn't stop you dying though,
like young David with those oxygen tubes, and his
pinched blue face. Poor old Laura, she must have felt it,
losing the only child like that. Probably wanted to ask
her all sorts of questions, any mother would, but say what
they liked they couldn't blame her. After all she'd been
very good to the boy, never asked to have him parked
on her, wouldn't have done if Grandpa hadn't died suddenly like that. No one else would take him on, not even

Edie for all her religion and you couldn't ship him back
in wartime, what with the *Lusitania* and the rest. He was a
nice enough kid tho' a bit dreamy, but she couldn't do
with sick people and when he was dying, well that put the
lid on it, too damned scaring. Of course she'd seen he had
the best that money could buy and the girls were in and
out of his room all the time, but the kid had noticed her
absence, asked for his Auntie Flo. She'd tried to stay with
him at the end, but it had frightened her too much—
time enough when one had to go oneself. She'd shocked
herself as she sat there wishing him dead to get it over,
and in the end she'd run out of the room. God knows
Laura would feel bitter if she knew, but Dr. Gladstone
understood how she had felt, he would tell Laura that
everything possible had been done. So long as those
bitches didn't gossip too much, everything would be alright, what the eye didn't see was a very true motto. All
the same she hoped to God there weren't many like herself, neglecting you when you were dying and wishing it
over. God, it frightened you to think about it, everything out of your hands and nothing to be done about it.
Still that wasn't the way to enjoy oneself. Thank God
the kids had started a bit of music, that would liven
things up. That elder boy of Edie's was struck on Ursula,
that would upset Edie, thought her children weren't
good enough, bad moral influence. She wouldn't trust
the girls alone with either of those boys, deep and dirty,
she knew the Sunday School type. "And how in the hell
can the old folks tell that it ain't gonna rain no mo'?"

So sang Flo, but Edie and her boys preferred "how in
the heck" and Laura who was sitting near to Edie just
left a blank. Stanley was the first to go to the old Joanna,
and when Edie's boys produced their ukeleles, everything was set for a really nice sing-song. A few jolly

choruses were always a help in breaking the ice, "Felix
kept on walking" made everyone laugh, especially when
Edie's younger boy walked up and down copying the
cartoon. Stanley was, as usual, slow to sense a change of
mood. "With his tail behind him" he laughed winking at
Edie, "well, I don't know where else he'd keep it". But
Edie was already regretting the slight looseness of their
earlier talk. "Don't be more of a fool than God made
you, Stanley" she snapped. Matters were not improved
when Flo's girl, Ursula, persuaded Edie's elder boy to
play for her. Ursula was certainly "fast" and she could
only be described as making "goo-goo eyes" as she sang
to her cousin "If you kiss a Ukelele lady, will you promise
ever to be true" and again "Where the tricky wicky-
wackies woo, if you like a Ukelele lady, Ukelele lady likea
you". Laura became worried at Edie's obvious restive-
ness, "Do sing us something Minnie" she cried "all these
modern things sound alike to me". She was to regret her
impulsiveness, as a moment later Harry moved up to the
piano to play "The Temple Bells" for his sister-in-law.
Soon Minnie's deep contralto filled the room, hooting
somewhat with the emotion of the words "I am weary
unto Death, O my rose of jasmine breath, and the month
of marriages is drawing nigh". Even Ursula was forced
to breathe "Oh that was lovely, Aunt Minnie. Sing some
more please", so Minnie gave them "Where My Caravan
has Rested" and "In the Heart of a Rose". Harry followed with his Cockney imitation of Albert Chevalier in
"My old Dutch", and though most of the family did not
follow his words, Laura's heart was glad at the compliment. Finally, Stanley got out his banjo and accompanied
himself with a soft strumming in "Oh dem Golden
Slippers" and "White Wings they never grow weary".
His low, light voice and the deep sentiment which he

lent to every word soon welded the party together in a mood of sleepy sadness.

Father used to sing these old songs so beautifully, thought Edie, how fine he used to look with his broad shoulders and his thick beard. God grant that my boys may grow up as their grandfather, always paying their way, asking nothing of any man, afraid to look no sinner in the face and call him to repentance, but always sweet and loving to their kith and kin as Father was. He had never been narrow like the Baptists, would sing these old songs so sweetly, though there never could be anything but sacred on Sundays. She had relaxed that rule with the boys, but sometimes she wondered if these changes were wise. Of course she did not want to be a spoilsport, liked them to have their motorbikes and their sports rifles, swimming and surfing too, even dancing. There was no harm in girls and boys playing games together, indeed there was a lot about the modern girl that she admired, more open and free, she liked the short skirts and the bobbed hair, but covering up the faces God had given them with paint and powder that was different. Pray God she did not allow her love for these boys to close her eyes to their weaknesses. Swearing or drunkenness, how often she had told them that there was nothing truly manly about these things. But they were good boys, they were her boys and grandfathers' boys, never smoked and only a glass of wine on a party occasion like this. All the same she wished in a way she had not brought them here, there could be no good in hearing the silly boastful weakness of her brothers-in-law, and as for her sisters-in-law they were bad, frivolous women: it wasn't the atmosphere she would have chosen for the boys. If it hadn't been that she had wanted to please Aunt Liz. . . . It was a thousand pities that Ursula was there, stupid little minx she would like to put her across her knee. So different from the girls that she hoped the boys would bring home one day, not yet of course, for the elder was only just twenty-one, but some day. A girl they had met out swimming or at the Chapel picnic on the Island. "Welcome to our home my dear" she would say to this daughter-in-law of hers, and afterwards as they sat sewing together on the porch, for such a girl would love to help Mother with the sewing, and the linen, she would look straight at her and tell her "I give you a husband, my dear, free from blemish, from evil thought or deed". They would come together spotless, and spotless they would grow beneath a loving Mother's eye. Yes, decidedly she would speak to that Ursula before any harm was done.

Edie had been sitting musing so long that there was general astonishment when her voice was suddenly raised above the general conversation.

"Now, my girl" she said to Ursula "you leave those boys alone. There's plenty of young fools to make sheeps' eyes at you down in the town, but good boys are scarce and I won't have you meddling with mine".

Ursula stared at her aunt for a moment, scarlet in the face, then rushed from the room, holding her handkerchief to her eyes. Edie's elder boy moved unhappily from one foot to the other, whilst the younger one sniggered at his brother's discomfiture.

"Ursula has no need to run after anyone, I can assure you" said Flo. "My God, I hope she can do better than cut some namby-pamby from his mother's apron strings".

"Go on, go on" said Edie in her driest tones "get it off your chest, woman, you'll feel better for it. But it won't alter the fact that my boys are not going to get mixed up with shameless girls like Ursula".

"Ursula's a decent, straightforward girl, not a damned,

creeping little toad, like your son. I heard about him making filthy suggestions to the youngest Palmer girl, and using the dirty bits in the Bible to do it".

"You're a very silly, angry woman" said Edie "who's saying things she doesn't understand. You had better put your own house in order before you go listening to wicked lies, neglecting the dying. . . ."

"What do you mean by that, may I ask?" queried Flo.

"Oh, don't be so silly, Flo" said Minnie. "You know very well what Edie means, we all do, except perhaps Laura, and if she doesn't it's high time she did".

The mellowing effects of the feast had worn off, leaving an irritation in every mind that was quick to flare up in anger. Already Stanley was telling Edie's sons that they should be ashamed to let their mother boss them about in public like that, to which his nephews retorted that such a remark was rich when every one knew Aunt Flo wore the trousers. Only Laura, bewildered by the undercurrents that were rising to the surface, had remained aloof. She could not however wholly disregard Minnie's remark.

"What ought I to know?" she asked coldly. "Why, that Flo neglected little David when he died, that she never went near the little fellow in his last illness" said Minnie speaking rapidly.

"It's a lie" shouted Flo dramatically "I swear it's a lie, Laura".

"The doctor has said that Flo did everything she could" said Laura, but she did not take Flo's outstretched hand.

"Well, of course, if you prefer to believe what strangers tell you" said Minnie.

"I choose to believe what the doctor told me, and in any case I think you've interfered in my affairs enough for to-day".

D

"Interfered in your affairs, what *do* you mean, Laura? Harry, I appeal to you, what *is* all this about?"

"I think you've appealed to Harry enough too for one day" said Laura with unconscious wit.

"Poor old Harry", said Minnie, laying her hand on his arm. "So this is the sort of life she leads you".

"Look here, Laura, you know" began Harry, but if Minnie was relying on male support for her victory, she was ignoring Laura's marital ascendancy.

"Now, Harry, that will do" she said. "*We* don't want to quarrel" and her husband was silenced.

The sense of unity was finally shattered, like Humpty Dumpty beyond repair. Nothing remained but to pack into the family Fords and Humbers, Wolseleys and Oldsmobiles and depart in mutual silence. Only Laura was left alone for a moment with Aunt Liz. "Thank you for a lovely party, Aunt Liz" she said.

The old lady came to consciousness from her gorged sleep, and by a strange chance recognized Laura for the first time that day.

"So you came to see us after all, Laura, they said you would, but I wasn't sure. People get so selfish being abroad, wrapped up in themselves. Well, you've aged a lot, but I don't suppose you're too old to learn from your family. The family doesn't meet often enough" she mumbled, sinking into her dozy state again "it does you all good, makes you think of something besides self for a bit."

Saturnalia

"I REALLY can't understand it" said Ruby Mann to her friend Enid "I thought things would have been humming long ago. Hi there" she shouted to the two medicos from Barts "a little action from the gang please". "It isn't a bit like the Mendel Court to be so slow. It's more like that morgue the Ventnor" Enid answered. Scrawny necked and anaemic, since childhood she had been drifting from one private hotel to another—She knew.

There was no doubt that the first hour of the staff dance had proved very sticky; servants and guests just wouldn't mix. Chef had started the evening in the customary way by leading out Mrs. Hyde-Green and the Commander had shown the young chaps the way to do it in a foxtrot with Miss Tarrant, the receptionist. But these conventional exchanges had somehow only created greater inhibitions, a class barrier of ice seemed to be forming and though a few of the more determinedly matey both of masters and men ventured from time to time into this frozen no man's land they were soon driven back by the cold blasts of deadened conversation. A thousand comparisons were made between this year's streamers and last year's fairylights; every measurement possible and impossible was conjectured for the length of the lounge; it would have verged on irony to have deplored even once more the absence through illness of the head waitress who had been such a sport the year before—by nine o'clock the rift was almost complete.

The manageress, Stella Hennessy, looked so pretty in

her dove grey tulle; with her soft brown hair and her round surprised eyes, she fluttered about like some moth with a genius for pathos—"a little bit of a thing" as Bruce Talfourd-Rich remarked, no one would have believed that she had a son at a public school. If *she* couldn't make things go nobody could. She had such grit and determination—never having sewn even a button on and then buckling to like this when the crash came. She was so exactly the right sort of person for the Mendel Court Hotel, thoroughly up to date and broadminded—One old colonel even went so far as to say that she was "O.T. Mustard", but then one heard afterwards that she'd been forced to put the poor old thing in his place. For there was no doubt that the Mendel Court was different to most other hotels in South Kensington—it was brighter, more easy-going, less fusty, less stuffy. They hadn't so many old tabbies and crocks with one foot in the grave. There was a poker set as well as a bridge set. Over half the residents were divorced or separated. Lots of them did interesting jobs, like being mannequins or film extras, or even helping friends to run night clubs, only showing how splendidly the right class of people could turn to when they had to. If they failed to pay their bills it was not from any ashamed indigence but because they thought they could get away with it.

It was something like a blow to prestige, then, when the dance seemed to hang fire. The lack of gaiety even disturbed Claire Talfourd-Rich, whose position as "injured wife" was so generally respected in the hotel that she could usually glide like Cassandra through any celebration. She looked strikingly injured to-night, her marble-white skin, and deep set dark eyes funereal against the heavy white silk ankle length gown with its gold wire belt. Bruce, too, was giving her every provocation with

Stella Hennessy—though to her trained eye it was clear
that Stella's babyish nagging would soon kill that affaire
—not that she any longer really noticed his infidelities,
her mind was too intent upon the cultivation of a
Knightsbridge exterior with a Kensington purse, but a
certain dull ache of self-pity at the back of her consciousness made her hold to the marriage with sullen tenacity.
To cry woe as you moved among the motley was one
thing, to form part of a group of hired mutes quite
another, and Claire soon found herself declaiming against
the failure of the evening to "get going". "It's too
shamemaking" she said in her deep contralto, she had
managed to get that new book *Vile Bodies* from the library
and was making full use of the Mayfair slang before it
was too widely known in S.W.7. "It'll be better soon
when all the old tabbies go to bed" said Enid, and sure
enough a moment later Mrs. Hyde-Green made prepara-
tions to depart. "I can't bear to tear myself away from
the fun" she said, and it was clear that she really meant it.
"But early to bed, you know. I'm sure *I* could do with a
lot more wealth" she added with a sigh. Soon she had
collected a party of the more staid around her to take a
last cup of tea in her sitting-room, for she was an old-
established resident and had three rooms with a lot of her
own furniture. Miss Tarrant, the receptionist, was
kindly included in the party, so that on the staff side, too,
there was a sense of relief. Only old Mrs. Mann declared
that she would stay to watch her daughter dance.

Mrs. Hyde-Green's departure saved the situation.
Liquor flowed freely and by ten fifteen, as Enid pointed
out, nearly everyone was a wee bit squiffy. Stella's eyes
were round with innocence as she called out to Claire in
her baby drawl. "What shall I do with this man of
yours? He keeps saying the most impossible things.

The trouble is, Mrs. Talfourd-Rich, that he's been too well taught". Only drink could have allowed her to let the bitch so far out of the bag. "Pipe down, Kiddie, pipe down" said Bruce, but Stella only giggled. "We're making rather an exhibition of ourselves, aren't we?" she said with delight. The pretty waitress Gloria had gone very gay "Take it away" she cried to the band. Her shoulder strap was slipping and a bit of hair kept flopping in her eyes. It was difficult to snap your fingers when your head was going round. She and young Tom the porter were dancing real *palais de danse* and "Send me, darling, send me" she cried. Bruce felt only too ready to oblige, he had no desire to stay with Stella all the evening if she was going to be difficult; these bitches were all the same after a bit. Soon he was dancing with Gloria, his shoulders moving exaggeratedly, for he prided himself on fitting in with all classes. "Send me" Gloria kept calling out. In the hinterland of old Sir Charles' mind some classroom memory earlier even than the glories of his colonial governorship was stirred. Waving a bridge roll unsteadily, his swivel eye fixed on the ceiling "The lady's repeated demands to be sent" he cried "remind me of the Hecuba. You know the lines" he said to Mrs. Mann. "It's funny" she replied "Ruby's the only one here with a bandeau to-night". No one was by to tell her that it would have been curious in 1925, but was far from strange in 1931. "Queen Hecuba, you know, in her distress asks to be taken away" Sir Charles continued "and then you get that wonderful accumulation of words in which the Greeks excelled. Labete, pherete, pempet', aeirete mou" he cried excitedly. "The old boy's three parts cut" said Bruce and he pressed Gloria closer to him. "We all think he's cuckoo" she giggled. "You know you're a very lucky girl to be dancing with a handsome man like me" Bruce continued, it was one of his favourite lines. "Says who?" Gloria cried. "Lovely maidens have cast themselves from high towers for my sake" he went on. Of course it was all silly talk, but you couldn't help liking him, he was good looking, too, with his little moustache, even if he was a bit old and baggy under the eyes.

Bertha, the crazy Welsh kitchenmaid with the bandy legs was dancing with page in a very marked manner. "I don't know what you young fellows are at" said Sir Charles to Grierson, the youngest student from Barts, "letting a boy of that age monopolize the women". Grierson protested that he was only two years older than page, but Sir Charles soon had him dancing with Bertha. "You're nice" she said, and years of yearning spent in institutions sounded in her voice "Press closer" she added and she rubbed her thighs against his. Sir Charles had no idea that page was an expert swimmer and he examined his life saving medal with keen interest. He himself was a daily Serpentine man. "The main thing is to keep practising your crawl" he said paternally.

Tom the porter's Irish glance had soon detected Stella's discomfiture. She was hot stuff alright, he thought, and then to be the friend of the manageress might be very useful. "You look beautiful tonoite, Mrs. Hennessy, if you'll pardon the familiarity" he said "That grey stuff—chiffon d'ye call it?—looks like the lovely sea mists". But Stella had fought too hard to maintain her class position to have it obscured by poetic words. In any case with her sexual flirtation was far too closely bound up with social ambition. "You've had more liquor than is good for you" her carefully lipsticked cupid's bow snapped at him, and her baby eyes were as hard as boot buttons. "Ye little God a'mighty bitch" he muttered.

"Ten Cents a dance that's what they pay me, gosh! how they weigh me down" the band played and Gloria sang with the tune. She was almost lying in Bruce's arms as he carried her through the slow foxtrot. Wouldn't it be wonderful, she thought, to be a dance hostess and to make your living dancing with hundreds of men every night. "Though I've a chorus of elderly beaux, stockings are porous with holes in the toes" she sang on, "I'm here till closing time, dance and be merry, it's only a dime". "By God that's a true song" said Bruce, choking slightly as he thought of the tragedy of it "Poor kids, what a god awful life dancing with any swine that likes to pay". Suddenly Gloria saw it like that too and she began to cry. "Bruce" she said "Bruce", and she buried her head in his shoulder. "There, there, baby" he replied soothingly.

Bertha's red curls danced in the air as she bobbed up and down holding young Grierson tightly to her, and her teeth showed forth black as ebony as she smiled at him. Cinderella had found her Prince Charming, the orphan girl's dream had come true. "What are you looking all round the room like that for, my sunshine boy?" she asked. "You don't want anything to do with that trollopy lot. Keep your eyes on me". From the horror of his fixed gaze she might have been the Medusa. Page, too, was staring in alarm at Sir Charles, as the old man's hand banged against his chest. "You'll have to broaden those shoulders, my lad". The old man was saying "You wait. They'll get you into uniform yet and teach you discipline. A bit of the barrack square that's what you need". Old Mrs. Mann kept smiling to herself. "I really think your mother's the tiniest bit geschwimpt" said Enid to Ruby—she had picked up the phrase on a Rhineland holiday. "Are you alright, Mother?" asked Ruby, but the old lady had turned to Claire Talfourd-

Rich, who was standing by her chair. "Isn't it a funny thing" she said "Ruby's the only one here with a bandeau to-night".

Tom the porter stared across at Claire. There was no doubt she was beautiful enough, with her dark eyes and her sleek black hair. She was a proud bitch alright, a different class altogether from that manageress. It would be something worth talking about to make her, and she'd be worth making too. "Would ye do me the honour of giving me a dance, madam?" he said, his Irish blue eyes all a-dancing, just the straightforward, sensible boy that he was. "That's very nice of you, Tom" drawled Claire "I should love to". "Did anyone ever tell you that you were a very fine dancer?" Claire asked, as half an hour later they were still waltzing together. "I think it's that beautiful look of yours in your lovely white dress that's brought out the lilt in me" Tom said, and he looked so straight at her that she felt that she couldn't be offended with the boy. You're in, Tom my boy, he thought, you're in.

Gradually, as drink broke down the barriers of self-consciousness, the classes began to merge. The servility of the staff began to give way to the contempt that they felt for the pretentious raffishness of their superiors. To the residents the easy moral tone of the staff was more surprising, for how were they to know that conditions of work in the hotel could only attract the scum of that great tide of labour which the depression had rolled into London. But like called to like. The Colonel's lady and Lily O'Grady were both "lumpen" under the skin.

Over the heads of the dancers, as they formed a circle to welcome 1932, floated the balloons, red, blue, green, silver, sausage shaped, moon shaped. Claire pressed Tom's hand tightly and her booming contralto sounded

above the other voices in "Auld Lang Syne". Bertha's
New Year resolution was a thick whisper in the ear of
young Grierson. Enid, who was nearby, started in sur-
prise for she thought she heard an awful word that ought
not to be spoken. Mrs. Mann's resolution, too, was
mumbled but she wanted, it seemed, more bandeaux worn
in 1932, whilst Ruby resolved never to go to another
dance. Sir Charles held a balloon in his hand "I trust
there will be greater comradeship in the coming year" he
said pompously. "Following the example of Achilles...."
but before he could finish his sentence the balloon burst
in his face to the sound of page's delighted giggles.
Bruce, sitting alone—for Gloria had gone for a moment
to you know where to adjust her shoulder straps—was
overcome by melancholy and resolved to have no more
to do with women. Tom caught at an old music hall
memory "Oi resolve to hang on to that beautiful rainbow
wherever I see't this year" he said, and remarked with
relief that the meaningless sentiment seemed what Claire
had expected from him. She leaned back, with her eyes
half shut, and, blowing smoke rings, she produced the
same smartly cynical resolution that she had used for the
five preceding years. "I resolve" she drawled "to do
good wherever I see a chance" and added with the same
perennial laugh "to myself", but somehow the flat little
cynicism seemed to have more meaning to her than ever
before. There really did appear to be something besides
clothes that might interest her, as she looked deep into
Tom's eyes. The hard, babyish tones of Stella Hennessy
interrupted their reverie. "I had no idea you were a
Socialist, Mrs. Talfourd-Rich" she said, her eyes great
circles of surprised blue. "You seem *quite* resolved to
break down class barriers. I shall have to make my New
Year resolutions about labour problems too" she added

curtly and she gave Tom a threateningly contemptuous glance.

But Stella Hennessy was to have more serious difficulties with the staff before the dance was over. A quarter of an hour later she passed the little waiting room in the annexe, on the way to her office. Through the half-open door she could see by the faint light of the window that there were two figures on the couch—Bruce lay half across Gloria, whose dress had fallen from the shoulders to reveal full breasts which he was fondling. Stella drew back to pass unobserved. Gloria began to giggle drunkenly "I s'pose this is what you do to old Mother Hennessy" she said. Bruce belched slightly "Christ" he said "that old cow! Why I'd rather squeeze milk out of a coco-nut". Stella felt quite sick; for a moment she almost doubted whether the drudgery of her life was worthwhile even to keep Paul at Malvern.

"If it's a crime, then I'm guilty, guilty of loving you" sang Tom in his low, crooning Irish tenor. "You're disgustingly handsome, you know" said Claire. After all there was nothing socially wrong about Lady Chatterly or Potiphar's wife so why not? "I'm dazzled to look at you, you're so beautiful" Tom replied. It was all so like a film that he felt quite carried away by his own words. "Ye've no roight to waste all that beauty" he went on. Breaking through the layers of social snobbery and imitated sophistication, dissipating even the thick clouds of self-pity which had covered her emotions for so many years, physical desire began to awake again in Claire. She thought of how often she had said that she only dressed to please herself, it's a bloody lie, she realized, I'd rather far dress to please men. "Will ye let me come to ye to-night?" said Tom hoarsely then he remembered with dismay that she shared a double room with Bruce.

"Oi'll show ye where ye can foind me, where we can be happy together." Through tears of pleasure Claire smiled at him. "Perhaps" she said "Perhaps". Across the ballroom Sir Charles was throwing streamers at page. "Fear wist not to evade as love wist to pursue" he intoned, but for once Francis Thompson was wrong, for when Sir Charles looked again page had disappeared through the green baize door to the service wing. "You're not dancing, Ruby" said old Mrs. Mann "and your bandeau's slipped, darling". "Blast the bandeau" cried Ruby, and tearing it from her head she threw it into the old lady's lap "I haven't danced the whole bloody evening" she cried and, in tears, she ran from the room. "I thought Ruby was a little overwrought" said her friend Enid. From the little service room near the dining hall there emerged a triumphant Bertha, leading a dejected Grierson. Her face was lit with happiness, life had given her all she asked. But young Grierson looked very white and as he approached the main staircase he was violently sick. "Steady the Buffs" called his fellow student from Barts. "Pardon me, Chaps, whilst I see old Jerry to bed".

"It would be stupid to talk to you about the kindness of the management, wouldn't it?" said Stella Hennessy, and her little rosebud mouth rounded as she spoke, making her look like a baby possessed by a malevolent devil. "Your class has never understood the meaning of gratitude. After this evening's disgusting exhibition you won't, of course, get the week's notice that you people are always talking about. I could send you away now, at once, but we will say tomorrow morning early. Do you hear me?" she said, suddenly raising her voice, for Gloria was staring so strangely "or are you too drunk?" Indeed the girl might have represented Drunkenness in a morality play as she sat opposite the office desk to which she had been summoned, the pink satin dress was half torn from her shoulders, pink artificial flowers and locks of brown hair fell alike across her face, her lipstick had smudged on to her cheeks, her tongue continually passed over her dry lips. Yet even in this condition she looked so young that Stella's face was suddenly distorted with rage and jealousy. "You filthy creature" and hysteria seized her. "Get out, get out" she screamed. Gloria rose with drunken dignity. "You silly old cow" she said, refinement giving way to full cockney. "You won't send me away, you won't, not on your ruddy life. I know too much about you, my treasure, old Mother have me if you like Hennessy". Bruce moved away from the frosted glass door of the office. It wasn't pleasant to hear women recriminating like that. He could not help resenting their apparent forgetfulness of himself in their hatred of one another. No place for men, he thought, as he moved slowly back to the dance floor.

Claire was standing by a pot of hydrangeas, the return of physical desire had animated her features as he had not seen them since the early years of their marriage. He walked over to her. "Hullo, Pookie" he said "care for a dance?" The use of her pet name after so many years came strangely to Claire, she knew quite well that his sudden interest was only an interval in the usual routine of their lives, she knew that there was no reciprocal feeling in herself, that she would regret the loss of her new hunger for Tom, but habit was very strong and it shut down upon her emotions, she could not resist an opportunity to strengthen the frayed marital tie. "Of course, darling" she said, stumping out her cigarette. When Tom came back with the whisky she had requested, he saw them dancing together—so that drunken fool had pushed his way in. "Now ye haven't forgot the dance ye promised me, Mrs. Talfourd" he said and he winked very slightly over Bruce's head. Claire never achieved such a successfully strangulated Knightsbridge tone as when she answered. "Oh Tom, how awful" she said "I'd quite forgotten. I haven't told you, darling" she said to Bruce "how sweet Tom has been in looking after me all the evening. But now this wretched husband of mine has deigned to turn up, I suppose I shall have to reward him by keeping an eye on him". "Thanks for looking after my old trouble and strife" said Bruce, as they moved away "I'll do the same for you some day, old man, come you're married". "Christ! the bitch" murmured Tom "and I thought I was in". There were only a few more dances before the band packed up, but everyone agreed that the Talfourd-Richs were the finest couple on the floor, indeed the evening would have been nothing without them. "Well after all" drawled Claire "if one can't put oneself out for the servants for *one* evening. It isn't very much to ask. Only *one* evening in the whole year". Sir Charles looked so miserable, as with a red paper crown on his head and a wooden rattle in his hand he prepared to go to his room. "Alas, yes, dear lady" he said, "The Saturnalia is at an end".

Realpolitik

JOHN HOBDAY sat on the edge of his desk and swung his left leg with characteristic boyishness. He waited for the staff to get settled in their seats and then spoke with careful informality.

"I know how frightfully busy you are. As a matter of fact I am myself", he said with the half-humorous urchin smile that he used for such jokes. Only his secretary, Veronica, gave the helpful laugh he expected. It was not going to be an easy meeting, he decided. "So I'm not going to waste your time with a lot of talk" he went on "I just thought. . . ." He paused and beat with his pencil against the desk whilst Mrs. Scrutton moved her chair fussily out of the sunlight. "Ready?" he asked with an over-elaborate smile "Right. Then we'll start again. As I was saying, we're all very busy, but all the same I thought it was time we had a little meeting. I've been here a week now and although I've had some very helpful chats with each of you in turn, we've never had a chance to get together and outline our plans". None of the three who formed his audience made any response. Veronica, who remembered him taking over new departments at the Ministry during the war, thought he hasn't got the right tone, he doesn't realize that he's coming up against deeper loyalties with these poeple, loyalties to scholarship and ideas. She almost felt like letting him fend for himself, but old habits were too strong.

"I'm sure it's what everybody's been wanting" she said in her deep voice. She had gauged rightly, his moment of uncertainty had gone, her faithful bark had guided him at the crucial moment. Mrs. Scrutton tried to discomfort him. She rustled the papers on her lap and whispered audibly to Major Sarson "Our plans. *His* plans for us would be more honest". But it was too late, she had missed her chance. John merely frowned at the interruption and it was Mrs. Scrutton who was left with burning cheeks, hiding her embarrassment by lighting a fresh cigarette.

"As you know" John went on, and Veronica could tell by the loud, trumpeting, rhetorical note of his voice that he was once more the confident salesman lost in the dream world of the grandiose schemes he was putting before them "I've got some very big ideas for the Gallery. I'm not an expert in any way as you people are, but I think that's possibly why Sir Harold's executors chose me for the job. They felt the Gallery had already got its full weight of scholars and experts, what it needed was a man with administrative experience, whose training had led him to take an over all view of things, to think, shall I say, widely rather than deeply. That's why they got me in. But I'm going to be absolutely frank with you" tossing a lock of brown, wavy hair from his forehead, he stared at his audience with a wide-eyed appeal "I need *your* help, without my staff I can get nowhere".

Major Sarson winced slightly. All this theatricality and the loud pitch of John's voice got on his nerves, besides he could feel a draught round his legs. It's like some damned Methodist preacher fellow, he thought.

"You've been grand in this first week" John went on "absolutely grand. I don't mind telling you now that when I arrived I was dead scared. You'd all been here for years, you knew the collections backwards, you had your own ways of running the place, and above all you'd had the inestimable advantage of knowing Sir Harold, of hearing exactly what was in his mind when he bought this picture or that object, of knowing what his ideals were in giving the public the benefit of his taste and experience. I felt sure you were bound to resent me as an outsider, and I knew I'd have done the same in your place".

The faces in front of him were quite unresponsive. He isn't going to get anywhere with sentimental appeals, thought Veronica, these people are idealists, there's nothing more hardboiled. The damned fools, thought John, they have the chance of turning this tin pot, cranky provincial gallery into a national institution and they won't play ball. Well if they can't see which way their own chances lie, they're not getting in the way of mine. They'll have to come to heel or go. His voice became a little sharper, a shade less ingenuous and friendly.

"You've all told me your views in our various little chats. Sometimes we've agreed, sometimes we haven't. You've inclined to the feeling that all is for the best in the best of all possible worlds, I've felt that some changes were needed, that the scope of the work here wanted broadening, that the organization wanted, let's face it, bringing up to date a bit, and in all this the Board has agreed with me".

Tony Parnell's baby face had grown steadily more pouting and scowling as John had been speaking. To think of this mountebank in charge of the Gallery, a professional careerist, who understood nothing of Sir Harold's ideas and aims, who had even laughed when he'd spoken to him of the metaphysical aspects of technique in painting. He had banked so much on becoming Curator. Sir Harold had spoken so often of him as "my torchbearer, the youngest member of our staff", and now these awful business men who had got control of the

E

estate had put this creature in. Major Sarson and Mrs. Scrutton were too old to fight these changes, he had promised before the meeting that *he* would make the challenge. Now was his opportunity. Red in the face, he opened his mouth, but in his nervousness his voice emerged a high falsetto. John smiled across at Veronica.

"The Board haven't had much opportunity of agreeing with us since they haven't heard our views" Tony squeaked.

"My dear Parnell" said John, and his tone was purposely patronizing and offensive. The old ones he regarded without rancour as dead wood to be cleared away, but Tony he disliked personally for his assumptions of scholarly disinterestedness and moral superiority. "Don't let that worry you. As soon as you've got your ideas clear come along and push them at the Board as much as you like. I shouldn't use too much of your favourite art jargon if I was you; the Board are anxious to help but they're only ordinary business men and they might not understand. If you follow my advice you'll come down to earth a bit, but of course that's entirely your affair".

Mrs. Scrutton fingered the buttons on her checked tweed coat nervously. "There's no need to bully Mr. Parnell" she said.

"Oh, come" said John jocosely "if Parnell's going to have the ladies on his side I shall have to surrender". To his delight he saw that Tony was frowning with annoyance.

"Do let me deal with this in my own way" he said to Mrs. Scrutton, whose lip began to tremble.

So that severe grey bobbed hair and man's collar and tie could dissolve early into tears, thought John, so much the better.

"Mrs. Scrutton was only trying to help you, Parnell"

said Major Sarson "Don't let us forget our manners, please".

John yawned slightly "When the little civil war's over" he said "I'd just like to outline our main functions. As I see them they're these: Relations with the Public, that's you, Parnell; Display, Mrs. Scrutton; Research, Major Sarson. Miss Clay" he indicated Veronica "is maid of all work. And I, well, I'm the Aunt Sally, ready to stop the bricks and pass on the bouquets".

Major Sarson looked at his watch impatiently. "I quite agree, with you, Major" said John "the sooner we get finished the better. No true gentlemen continue to hold meetings after opening time". The old man's face twitched violently, no one before had referred overtly to his notorious weakness.

"I'd like to take the public first" said John. "You've done a first-rate job, Parnell—within its limits. But you haven't gone far enough. You've got real enthusiasm and that's half the battle—but only half. You give the public first-rate value in lectures and catalogues when they get here, but you don't try to get them to come. I know what you're going to say 'They'll come if they're interested'. But aren't you being a bit hard on the poor, tired, pushed around public of to-day? They've got to be told about the place. You've got to compete with the cinema, the football team *and* the fireside radio. In short you've got to advertise and you can't do that unless you have figures". Here John paused and picked up a file of papers.

"You have all the figures there" said Tony sulkily.

"I know" said John "but don't you think they're just a bit too general? 'So many people visited the Gallery on August 5th, so many on November 3rd'. But what sort of people? Who are we catering for? Were they Chinamen, shopgirls, farmers, or just plain deaf-mutes? To tell us anything these figures want breaking down into groups —so many foreigners, so many over-forties, so many under-twenties. That's the way to build up a picture. Now supposing you run over these figures in the way that I suggest and we'll talk again".

Tony was about to protest that this task was impossible, but John held up his hand. "No, no, time's very short and there's one more point I want to raise before we pass on to display". Mrs. Scrutton drew her coat tightly round her. "It's about the lecture room. Sir Louis Crippen was saying something at the last Board meeting about its not being free for his archaeological society when he needed it. Do you know anything about that?"

Tony Parnell hesitated. "Well, actually" he said "Mrs. Scrutton makes all the lecture hall arrangements".

"But isn't it the P.R.O's pigeon?" asked John.

"Yes" said Tony "but . . . well . . . Mrs. Scrutton. . . ."

"I see" said John coldly. "Perhaps you'd enlighten me, then, Mrs. Scrutton".

The grey bob shook as she answered, an involuntary shake that was to prove the prelude to age's palsy. "Sir Louis asked for Tuesday and Tuesdays are always booked by Miss Copley" she said.

"Miss Copley?"

Mrs. Scrutton guessed that he knew the answer and her reply attempted a rebuke. "Miss Copley is an old and true friend to the Gallery" she said. "She's been giving her lectures to Schools on Tuesdays for many years".

"No doubt" said John "but I still think Sir Louis should have preference".

"I don't agree at all" said Major Sarson "it would be most unfair".

"Yes, why should Sir Louis receive special treatment?" asked Mrs. Scrutton.

"Well, frankly," replied John "because although Miss Copley may be a very old friend, Sir Louis is a very influential one and the Gallery needs influential friends".

Before Mrs. Scrutton there floated Sir Harold's features, like Erasmus she had thought him, the last of the humanists. Major Sarson too, remembered his old friend's handshake and his firm clear voice "Sarson" he had said "this money came to me through false standards, false distinctions. There shall be no distinctions in its use but those of scholarship". The eyes of both these old people filled with tears.

John turned to Veronica. "You've nothing to do, Miss Clay" he said. "In future you will take on the lecture hall arrangements. Anything important you'll refer to me". Mrs. Scrutton made a gesture of protest. "No, no" said John. "I'm not going to let you wear yourself out on these minor details, you're far too valuable to the Gallery. Besides, you've got more than a full time job with Display if it's properly carried out".

Tony Parnell half rose from his chair "I thought the Lecture Hall arrangements came under Public Relations?"

"So did I" said John "until you disillusioned me".

"Next we come to Display. I suppose no side of our work has been more revolutionized in recent years. The Philadelphia report, you know, and the Canadian Association series" he went on, smiling at Mrs. Scrutton. She suddenly felt very tired, she had seen these documents but had never been able to bring herself to read them. "But there's no need for me to mention these things to you" John continued. "Your arrangement of the miniature collection" and he sighed in wonder. "Well, I'm going to pay you a great compliment there. Your arrangement of the miniatures not only makes one

want to look at them, it makes it impossible for one not to
look at them. I'm sure, Mrs. Scrutton, you'll agree with
my wish that some other sides of the collection had the
same advantages as the miniatures—the jewellery, for
instance, and the armour. But that's not your fault.
There's just too much for one person, that's all there is to
it. The same applies to the research. I'm not going to
embarrass Major Sarson by talking about his position as a
scholar" he waved his hand towards the old man who
went red round the ears "suffice it to say what we all
know, that the Gallery is honoured by the presence of the
world's greatest authority on the Dutch school, and a
great scholar of painting generally. Though I doubt, by
the way, whether the Major's exactly fond of the moderns.
I sometimes wish that the Gallery possessed only paint-
ings, I'm sure Major Sarson does. Unfortunately that
isn't the case. I fully sympathized with him when he
spoke to me as he did of 'those wretched pots and pans,'"
here John laughed patronizingly "but I doubt if a
ceramics man would. Frankly" he said, turning to Major
Sarson "I consider it disgraceful that a scholar of your
calibre should be taken off your real work in this way.
Now how, you may ask, do I suppose to remedy the
situation? Well the answer is that I propose to treble the
staff. From next month new staff will begin to arrive—
some students from the Universities, some more ex-
perienced men from other galleries and museums".

There was silence for a minute, then Mrs. Scrutton
spoke. "Does the Board know of this?"

"Yes" said John "they fully approve the scheme".

"Do they realize the expense involved?" asked Tony,
the practical man.

"The Board are business men" said John "they know
that outlay must precede returns." He looked round at

their faces. "Well, I think that's all" he said. "I know you will give the new members of the staff the same co-operation you have given me, whether it is a question of instructing and training them, or in some cases of working under them". His tone was openly sarcastic.

"Do I understand that people will be put over us?" asked Mrs. Scrutton.

"In cases where experts are brought in, it may be necessary to make revisions in seniority" said John.

"You realize, of course, that in such an eventuality we should resign" said Major Sarson.

"That would be a great loss to the Gallery, but we could not, of course, control your decisions" replied John, and opening the door, he bowed them out.

"Golly" said Veronica "you do tell some lies, don't you? Or have the Board ratified your staff changes?"

"How many more times must I tell you, Veronica, that truth is relative" said John.

Veronica looked down for a minute "I'll make you some coffee" she said.

"Yes" said John "Victory always makes me thirsty. I cannot help being satisfied when I think of the well merited unpleasant few weeks those three are going to have. The punishment of incompetence is always satisfactory".

"Mmm" said Veronica doubtfully.

"What's that mean? You've not fallen for this senti-mental stuff about Sir Harold, have you?"

"Good Lord, no" said Veronica. "It's not those mis-fits I'm worrying about, its you."

"Me?" said John. "Why?"

"You're getting too fond of bullying" said Veronica "it interferes with your charm, and charm's essential for your success". She went out to make the coffee.

What Veronica said was very true, thought John, and he made a note to be more detached in his attitude. All the same these criticisms were bad for his self-esteem. For all her loyalty Veronica knew him too well, got too near home. Charm was important to success, but self-esteem was more so. His imagination began to envisage further staff changes, perhaps a graduate secretary would really be more suitable now.

A Story of Historical Interest

IT was clear, thought Lois, that no real provision was
made in these ambulances for relatives, of the deceased
she was about to say, but recovered herself in time, of
the sick, of course. My legs are quite stiff, she thought,
and my bottom will never be the same again after sitting
for so long on this little bench. How selfish! how
dreadfully selfish to think of oneself when Daddy was
lying there dying, or at any rate possibly dying, for no
one, not even the doctor seemed to know whether he
would recover from the effects of this stroke. His face
looked so strange, almost blue grey, and at intervals he
was sick into the little white bowl which she or Harold
held up to him—not really sick, she thought, remembering with horror those bouts of vomiting she had under-
gone as a child after parties,—this wasn't like that at all,
just a thin, watery fluid with globules of green phlegm
floating in it. His hand, too, constantly brushed feebly
at his face or picked at his lips, as though he was removing
an imaginary cobweb. He was more comfortable now,
though, since they had had the nurse to wash him.

Perhaps the most awful moment of the three awful
days, since she had been summoned back to the hotel
from the office, had been the realization of her own
clumsiness and of the pain she was causing him when she
had tried to wash him on that first afternoon. The thick
hairs had got coated together and stuck to the body with
sweat and urine, and she had pulled at them in her efforts
to sponge him. His eyes had gleamed red and small with
hatred as he had cursed her for it; "God damn you, you

bloody bitch" he had said again and again, for he was impatient of any pain and behind it all, though she tried hard not to believe it, terrified of dying, angry like a trapped animal. She had gone on relentlessly, however, hoping that at such times it was necessary to be cruel to be kind. It had angered her, too, for she longed to show him her tenderness, to envelop him in a deep, almost maternal love, but by her blundering roughness she had failed. She had hated him for underlining her clumsiness; if he had not been cowardly and inconsiderate she would never have guessed at her failure.

How different the nurse had been! She could still see those "frank" Irish eyes with their sly, sexy twinkle, could hear that soft brogue jollying him on, whilst the plump hands moved him about like a baby, turning him over, powdering him, making him easy. "It's a wicked boy ye've been, I can see, and will be again. Ye've not finished with the poor girls yet with those great eyes of yours" and her father's chuckle, sensual still though feeble. "What do you know about me and the girls, nurse? I'd like to know". She had seen herself suddenly as Mummy, awkward, unattractive, without gaiety; and the nurse as a symbol of those other women who had made up the pattern of his life. It seemed so unfair that the drab, clumsy part of her which came from her mother should have made its appearance at that moment, putting her at a disadvantage, alienating him from her as he was fading out of life. Ever since Mummy's death she had suppressed that side of herself, had deliberately cultivated gaiety, had flirted with him to hold him at home as she felt Mummy should have done—and she had succeeded so that he had said she was "the nicest kid he'd ever run around with", called her "Daddy's little pal". She could hear her own voice now as she spoke to the nurse, prim and tense like an affronted governess: "Mr. Gorringe has never been very fond of women's chatter, nurse, so I expect you'll find him rather impatient. It's only a question really of keeping him comfortable. I'd have taken it on myself but we don't know how long the illness will last and I can't stay away from work indefinitely". "Not fond of women now Oi'm surprised to hear't with his little twinklin' eyes. But it's merciful you got a nurse in when you did, the poor thing's been pulled about cruelly". She had almost struck the bitch. Nevertheless she had been just: Daddy needed a nurse and so the nurse should stay. No, it was only that dreadful letter which had made it imperative to dismiss her.

When Nurse appeared dressed for the street Lois felt a greater antipathy even than before. Really, she thought, she's no better than a little shopgirl, an "amateur pro". She had seen such little creatures with their black hair, badly put on lipstick and insolent eyes, hanging on the arms of soldiers in the Edgware Road. The sort of horrible women whose full animal natures only appeared when they were drunk, singing and shouting obscenities on the tops of buses. What an unsuitable person to be Daddy's nurse, and she thought of those brown leather wallets of his smelling of lavender water and packed with letters from the women of his past,—clever, beautiful women,—actresses, wives of friends, models, all the distinguished bric-à-brac of Edwardian wild oats. How degrading that at such a time he should be making moribund passes—I didn't mean those words, she thought with shame, they just slipped into my mind— flirting with a cheap Irish wanton. "A nice, reliable girl" Doctor Filby had said, he must be insane. And then into

her mind came other incidents—Daddy leaving her with
an excuse at Leicester Square to speak, as she well knew,
to a hardfaced, peroxide prostitute; Mummy finding that
cretinous Welsh housemaid in bed with him; that nurse-
maid who appeared on the stairs with her hair down,
laughing, and shouting curses at Mummy—My God, she
thought, perhaps it isn't so unsuitable after all. I'm
allowing myself to dramatize the situation, she decided,
after all I'm very overtired. The girl's private life is no
concern of ours, she's a good competent nurse and she
makes Daddy comfortable that's all that matters.

"Won't you have a cup of tea before you go, Nurse?"
she asked.

"Well now that's kind of you. I'll not say no". Really,
the girl had a most pleasant smile.

They sat uneasily in Lois' room while the kettle boiled
on the gas-ring.

"Yours must be a tiring life, Nurse" said Lois, at last,
in dead tones. "But then I expect you wouldn't have
taken up nursing unless you had felt a great call to it. I
mean it always seems to me to be a vocation rather than a
profession". What a flat, Kensington platitude, she
thought, and oh my God! the girl's probably a Catholic,
and she'll think it blasphemous to say "vocation".

"It is grand work indeed to feel that you can help the
poor things in their trouble" Nurse replied. I am a fool,
thought Lois, always seeing depths in people where they
don't exist.

"We shall all have need of you" she said "if war comes.
That is if any of us are left alive after the first hour".

"Do you think it'll come to war then?" said the nurse,
and her voice took on a sudden excited note, accentuating
the brogue. "God in heaven, I pray not. But they do say
they have the coffins ready for us, in their thousands, and

made of cardboard too, such terrible massacres they're expecting. Mind you, if it came it would be a righteous war, they've been doing the devil's work there in those concentration camps. But there's worse than that they've done, dividing father against son, destroying homes".

Really, thought Lois, I thought I was covering an awkward silence and I've let loose the Abbey Theatre. Aloud she said:

"I can see you feel very strongly about it, Nurse. I wish I could feel as certain as you, but the papers are so lying, one doesn't know what to believe".

"Oh if my brother could hear you say that, it's what I'm always telling him. He's turned a Red" she said in a hushed whisper "and they'll no more receive him at home. He fought in Spain with that dreadful International Brigade. It was fighting against God I told him, but he only laughs. He's for ever speaking of the dreadful things the Fascists did at Barcelona and such places. 'It's the truth I'm telling you' he says, but how can one believe him? Oh why can't they leave us alone?" and to Lois' ear she seemed almost to be wailing "don't we have our own private thoughts that are aching in us?"

She was silent for a few minutes and Lois suspected that she was embarrassed at her outburst, then putting down her empty cup, she handed Lois a blue envelope. "I must be going" she said. "Will you give this to Doctor Filby, please, it's a note of the patient's temperature. You'll be sure to give it to him?" she added. "Of course" said Lois. How hysterical she seems for a nurse, she thought, and then felt unjust, after all, she too, was probably overtired.

After the nurse had left, Lois returned to sit in her father's room. She felt overwrought after the alarm of yesterday and the first sleepless night of sitting by the sickbed. Nothing has changed, she thought, as she lay back in the armchair—the rows and rows of brown, highly polished shoes each with its shoetree; the ivory and silver brushes and combs with the Gothic monograms; the silver framed photograph of her parents taken on their honeymoon, and a later one of Mummy in a chiffon blouse with a cameo brooch—all these were objects of familiar vision: and she could guess at so many others—the neatly pressed grey check suits on their hangers; the stovepipe trousers of the old Edwardian narrowness, some even with shoestraps; the two grey bowlers which he was so proud to display in these degenerate, sloppy days; the photographs of Duke Rodney, his champion bulldog—everything smelling of his beloved lavender water. That familiar scent filled the room, closing all round her in her drowsiness, but behind it there was another scent, sharp, acrid, disgusting. Suddenly she was roused from the sleep that was enveloping her—for a moment she had been forgetting the awful thing that had happened, but that scent had recalled it—the sharp stench of vomit, the faint, sickly odour of faeces. That was why the room was so unbearably hot, why, although sunlight was pouring in through the windows, the gasfire was burning at full height. The stroke that had robbed Daddy of the power to move his legs, had left him perpetually numbed, so that he who had so loved fresh air seemed always to be complaining that the room was cold.

Stroke was a well chosen name, she decided, for it had descended upon them so suddenly, out of the void, shattering their happiness. She had suffered moments of apprehension that such a blow would fall ever since Daddy had passed his seventieth birthday, but he was so active and gay, and people lived to such an age nowadays, that she had always put the thought from her mind. She was too busy understanding him, letting him do what he wanted and preventing Harold from hearing of it. That was what had aged him, she felt no doubt of it, feeling dependent on Harold for his money. *She* never allowed him to feel that the little bit he got from her was anything but his own. But Harold was always grumbling at the way the money was spent, just like Mummy had done. *She* understood Daddy better than that, he was like a naughty child; of course he'd always been spoilt, but he was so sweet when he had his own way. He wanted the good things of life, needed the excitement of gambling. Harold was such a horribly *good* man, he never wanted to do anything he shouldn't. It was true he would pay Daddy's debts, but always with such a long face and sometimes even with a lecture. It hurt Daddy's pride so, and she couldn't bear to see him humiliated at his age, so that she was always interceding for him, pretending the money was needed for the household, getting at Harold when Daisy was not there. It was Daisy really who was so unkind, she who was not even one of the family, except by marriage. They were always suggesting that Daddy should live with them at Tunbridge Wells; but he would have hated it, away from the West End, his poker and his racing, treated like an old dependant. She and Daddy had fought them and had won. "You don't want to be rid of your old Daddy, do you, Lois?" he had asked, after one of Daisy's visits, and she had knelt on the floor by his side, rubbing her cheek against his poor, worried face, running her fingers through his hair. "Silly" she had said "I must have my old Daddy to bully or what should I do when I was cross?" But now that this awful thing had happened, how were they to meet it? She could not afford to leave her job and who would look after him in a hotel? No one would say whether the paralysis was permanent. They would take him away from her, put him with the incurables. No! O God! No, rather let him die than that, she said half aloud, and for a moment she fancied that the drawn face on the pillow had smiled at her. Perhaps he would recover, perhaps it was only a temporary thing, a warning for the future. Oh God! let him recover, and we will take such care not to offend again, she murmured. If only he could move about even a little they could carry on as before. The main thing was to know what was happening. That nurse knew, she had probably written it all in the letter—"Mr. Gorringe has only three days to live". They had no right to ignore her so, it was bad enough to treat poor Daddy like an animal to be ordered about at will, just because he could not move, but *she* could not be treated so, she was still able to protect him. She picked up the blue envelope and tore it open. Nothing was written on the notepaper but temperature recordings and the times at which medicine had been given. She flung the paper down in disgust, and then on the reverse she saw what seemed to be a private letter—"What's eating you, honey?" she read. "It's over four weeks and more that I've never seen you, and none of my letters getting an answer. Darling you know I'm mad about you. I can't sleep for thinking of it. When shall I see you again? You know where you can find me and I think you know I can make it worthwhile to you. For God's sake give me a break, Fil. Kath." "Private thoughts that are aching in us" thought Lois, My God, how disgusting!

The ambulance lurched slightly as it avoided a careless cyclist. Mr. Gorringe's shoulders seemed to heave as he retched again, the green globules slipping down his beard in snail tracks. Lois wiped his chin with a hand towel. She could hear him murmuring faintly "I'm very ill, God help me, I'm very ill", and his eyes stared with fright as his body shook at a sudden hiccough. Harold held up the basin, "Poor old chap" he whispered to Lois "He's so very helpless". Lois pretended not to hear; it was just what Mrs. Cooper had said at that awful interview in the hotel office—the interview that had finally sent Daddy from her. After the first moments of fury, she could have disregarded that disgusting cheap letter, have treated the nurse and Doctor Filby as though she had never read it, or at the worst doctor and nurse could have been changed, but Mrs. Cooper's statement had been so final, so irrevocable.

There were residents at the St. Mary Abbot's Hotel who said that Mrs. Cooper's office was the most spacious room in the house and on this warm July afternoon their belief would have seemed amply justified. It was more of a sitting room than an office with its rich lacquer suite from Maples, the noticeably antique grandfather clock and the Edwardian curio-table containing silver spoons and ostrich eggs. On this particular afternoon the room was a riot of blue—delphiniums, lupins, love in the mist and anchusa all brought from Mrs. Cooper's country home near Midhurst—for Mrs. Cooper loved blue, it was "her colour", with her baby blue eyes and her carefully waved white hair she felt sure that "blue suited her" as her turquoise earrings and butterflywing brooch could attest. Lois always felt at a disadvantage with Mrs. Cooper; the hard eyes, the drawling voice, with its occasional glottal stop betraying an East End origin, seemed to

F

assert success and comfortable security, to underline her own genteel penury. She hated to think that this vulgar woman knew so exactly Daddy's financial vagaries, had even refused him little loans to meet gambling debts. This afternoon's summons to the office had completely unnerved her, cutting through her private grief, overwhelming even the horror of that disgusting letter. It was so unlucky that Mrs. Cooper should happen to be there, for in these last years a rising bank balance had taken her on cruises to Norway and to Greece, on trips to Monte and Bordighera and Biarritz, leaving more malleable manageresses as vicereines, but 1939 had brought an uncertainty that daunted even her.

"Sit yourself down, Miss Gorringe" said Mrs. Cooper "I don't think you've met my nephew" and she waved her hand towards an overdressed young man with a Ronald Colman moustache.

"Pleased to meet you" said the nephew.

"Now, Tony, you great lump" said Mrs. Cooper "stir yourself and get Miss Gorringe a cigarette".

"No thank you" said Lois, and she thought Pray God that he goes soon. Why should I have to hear their conversation when Daddy's so ill? She will try to separate us and I am determined to fight her, but if I have to talk about other matters I shall lose my resolution. She has done it on purpose to break my nerve.

"I've just been telling this boy that if things go on like this he'll have to be measured for a uniform" said Mrs. Cooper. "We'll have you in khaki yet, Tony" she added with a laugh.

"If things come to a head I shall join the Air Force" said the young man.

"You'll go where they send you, my lad" said his aunt. "Hitler means war, you mark my words".

"I can't believe he can be so crazy" said Lois.

"Can't you?" replied Mrs. Cooper "I can. Well, Tony, give my love to mother. See you next month, Hitler willing".

At last he has gone, thought Lois, now I must be firm. Attack is the best defence.

"I'm so glad you asked to see me, Mrs. Cooper" she said "I was intending to come down anyway. There are one or two things my father will be wanting now that he is ill".

"Yes?" said Mrs. Cooper, without appearing to hear, then she said rather distinctly. "You'll miss him, won't you, Miss Gorringe? But Tunbridge Wells isn't far, you'll be able to run down whenever you want to. Has your brother made arrangements yet?"

"My brother couldn't possibly accommodate my father" said Lois firmly.

"Couldn't he? What a pity! Well, I expect he'll find a nearby nursing home".

"Daddy wouldn't like that at all. He values his independence so much. Besides" Lois added ingratiatingly. "He's so fond of the hotel".

"And we're so fond of him" said Mrs. Cooper. "He's the nicest guest I've got. You tell him that from me, it'll cheer the old dear up. Don't worry, my dear, they often rally from these strokes, but he'll be an invalid, of course. He couldn't possibly get the attention he needs in a hotel. Poor old chap, he's so very helpless".

"But we've got a nurse" said Lois.

"Now, my dear Miss Gorringe, do you imagine I'd ever keep any maids if all the guests had nurses in attendance? You know as well as I do how badly that class get on with each other. Why! there's been trouble already. No, you make other arrangements; shall we say not later than a week from to-day?" and Mrs. Cooper turned to her account book.

"Aren't you rather presuming?" began Lois.

Mrs. Cooper laid down her fountain pen and her smiling blue eyes were quite unflinching. "No, my dear, I'm not" she said sweetly. "The situation's quite impossible. You're tired out or you'd see the point at once. You take my advice and ring your brother up now. Doctors can be very callous sometimes, they see so many of these cases, of course. It would be a pity if he insisted on sending your father to the hospital, it's so difficult to get them out once they're there", and she returned to her accounts.

The movement of the ambulance had become faster but yet more smooth. Lois guessed that they had reached the open country. Mr. Gorringe was seized with a new bout of hiccoughs, great shaking, bursts of wind that seemed to rack his whole frame. His cheeks were flecked with green, and dull white patches appeared on his cheekbones which reminded Lois of his appearance in a fit of rage. It was quite possible, she thought, that he *was* in a rage; he kept murmuring, but the words were too faint to be understood. She helped Harold to prop his body forward with the pillows, whilst the attendant wiped his forehead. His face was suffused with sweat after the exertions caused by the hiccoughs and Lois noticed that the sweat smelt rank, almost as though the body was putrefying. At last the bout came to an end, and he lay back, exhausted and snoring. Harold looked apprehensive "I don't like that stertorous breathing at all" he whispered, but soon the patient was sleeping more quietly. "I don't want to say anything against Dr. Filby, but I shall be glad when Doctor Grimmett sees the old man. Filby's diagnosis seems so vague, in fact his whole handling of the case wants a bit of explaining. Oh! don't think I'm complaining" he continued as he saw a shadow cross his sister's face. "You've done your best in a very nasty jam, but I think it was just as well the old man was moved when he was". The awful thing is, thought Lois, that I can't defend myself. Dr. Filby's whole behaviour was most unsatisfactory, he never really came to the point, but what could I have done? If Harold knew of that letter from the nurse he'd make an awful row. She noticed that the bedclothes had slipped away from the patient's feet, and, as she tucked them in, she saw again the strange, brown scabs on her father's legs. The whole of that perplexing unsatisfactory interview with the doctor came back to her.

They sat in the corner of the lounge in great deep armchairs, so that Lois was forced to perch on the edge in order to hear what he said. She felt all the time as though she was slipping off the seat. It's absurd that he should look so like a stage doctor, she thought, with his well cut morning coat, and striped trousers, with that bronzed, handsome face and strong jaw, and crowning all, the iron grey wavy hair of the matinée idol. As the interview progressed she found herself wondering at moments whether he was not, in fact, an actor and no real doctor at all, so exactly right was the form of his speech and yet so tenuous and vague was the information it contained. "Impostor deceives Kensington girl" she thought but that was absurd. She really must listen more carefully to what he was saying and she tried to set her face as she did when Harold talked to her about the workings of the Special Jury System or Daddy about Rugby Union Rules.

"Of course it's rather difficult to be specific when one doesn't come into the case until this late stage" he said.

Oh dear! thought Lois, he's offended. Aloud she said.

"He's not consulted anyone else, Doctor Filby", but judging by its result the apology did more harm than good.

"I imagine not" said Dr. Filby coldly. "The legs are entirely paralysed, of course, but that is not necessarily a permanent condition".

"You mean you think he may recover" said Lois.

"He might well improve" said Dr. Filby. "He's not young, of course. Poor old chap, he keeps his sense of humour, doesn't he? We can all do with that in these days". Lois laughed obediently. "And if he doesn't get better, will he linger on like this for long?" she asked.

"I should think he must have had a little stroke before this. Can you remember anything of the kind?" said Doctor Filby. "Of course these attacks are often so slight that they pass off without much notice". Lois thought for a moment. "He had a bad giddy spell at the club some six months ago" she said. "Very likely" said the doctor "I understand movement has been difficult at times". "He shuffles more than he used to" Lois replied "and sometimes his legs seem to run away with him. But then he's over seventy and up to now he's been so active and cheerful". He isn't listening to what I'm saying she thought, he doesn't even seem to be listening to himself, he's quite abstracted, it's really hopeless to talk to him. I shall make one more serious effort to get some information. "Do you think he's dying, Doctor Filby?" she asked. "If so, don't be afraid to tell me". "He's in a bad condition" said the doctor "I'll send a nurse round, a nice, reliable girl, you'll like her. No meat or eggs, I think. Otherwise let him rest, he'll sleep a lot". "I know names and that sort of thing aren't important" said Lois "but I should like to be able to give my brother some exact statement. He's a bit fussy, you know" she added apologetically. Dr. Filby laughed. "No meat or eggs" he repeated. "The kidneys are affected. There's definite albumen in the water. I suppose your father was a bit wild when he was younger. You'll excuse my asking but do you know of any V.D. story?" "I've never heard of anything" said Lois. "I'm just a bit puzzled by those marks on his legs" said the doctor. "There's a possibility of a tertiary syphilis, but don't worry about it, even if it is so, it can only be of historical interest." "Are there any medicines I should get, Dr. Filby?" Lois asked. "These hotels must be very comfortable" said the doctor "but a bit gloomy at times" and he shivered. "Nurse'll look after any medicines. In a few days' time we can see how he is and then if necessary I'll get him admitted to hospital". "Do you mean to give him treatment then?" Lois asked. "Hardly that" said Doctor Filby . "But he may live on for a long time yet you know, and he'll need hospital attention". At last he's given a straight answer, thought Lois. How dare he suggest putting Daddy in a hospital ward like that, among the incurables probably? How dare he? how dare he? "Oh my brother and I couldn't permit that" she said. "My father would eat his heart out with misery in a public ward". "I'll write a note for the matron and get them to put a screen round the bed". I *must* stop this, thought Lois, or I shall hit him. How dare he talk to me like this just because we're not rich? He treats us as though we were working class people. "If it's necessary for my father to be moved" she said "he will, of course, go to my brother's place, but I shall have to feel very convinced that the move is necessary". Once more Doctor Filby reverted to the indirect

answer. "I'll look in to-morrow morning" he said "about
eleven. We're going through difficult times" he added
"but I think Chamberlain's doing his best. I'd like to see
what some of these critics would do if they were in his
shoes". Lois felt that she too had a right to be abstracted
now, so she merely replied "Yes". "Well" said Doctor
Filby "Good-bye. Don't worry. And don't sit too much
in this lounge, it's like a funeral parlour".

Mr. Gorringe was sleeping peacefully at last, though
now and again he would wake at some jar in the movement of the ambulance and give vent to a mumbled obscenity. "I hope the old man doesn't start cursing Miss
Wheeler" said Harold. "We're almost there now". "I
don't think I should worry" said Lois "they're probably
used to that sort of thing at the Nursing Home". "Oh!
she's a good old sort" said Harold "I don't suppose
she'll bat an eyelid, but still she *is* doing us a kind turn
really and then she's got all the children to consider".
"All the children? I don't understand, Harold". His
voice in explanation was worried and apologetic. "Look
old dear, I haven't had the time to tell you about this end,
but we've had a dickens of a time finding anywhere that
will take the old man. The nursing homes are simply
nests of robbers, they want ten or twelve guineas a week,
and even then one doesn't hear anything too good about
them. Anyhow I won't beat about the bush with *you*.
Business is at such a standstill with all these crises, people
just won't take a risk, I simply feel I can't afford to lay
out a sum like that as things are now. After all it may be
for a long time. The old man'll probably get much better,
he may hang on for a couple of years, but he'll need
proper attention. Miss Wheeler's just the person for

him, Daisy thinks no end of her. She's a trained nurse, of course" he said proudly. "She'll look after him like a child. But it *is* rather a favour, because, you see, normally she only takes babies and things—children that aren't wanted, you know, poor little blighters. Awfully nice kids, I saw some of them the other day. I should say she made them very happy" he added.

"How gratifying to hear" said Lois savagely.

"Of course she wouldn't do this for everyone" continued Harold "but Daisy's won her heart as usual. They've worked together on some Conservative Committee".

Thank Heaven Harold never recognizes sarcasm, thought Lois, I won't lose my temper, I won't, I won't, for Daddy's sake. It may be some time before I can move him and I don't want any unpleasantness. I'll never forgive them, never. Darling Daddy they shan't treat you like this and go unpunished. Aloud she merely said "We'll have to see how it works, won't we, Harold?"

Her brother was buoyant again at once. "I'm sure it's just the thing. Daisy's up to her eyes at the minute trying to jog the local party into action, but you can rest assured, Lois, she'll see that everything's up to standard. By the way" he went on somewhat timorously, "you won't see her at Miss Wheeler's. She's got a very important committee meeting on, and there didn't seem much point in her coming down anyway. I mean the less there are to get in Miss Wheeler's way the better" he ended lamely. It suddenly struck Lois that he thought she would mind Daisy's absence more than the muddle about the nursing home. How fantastic! "That's all right, Harold" she said "I understand", and then she began to laugh wildly, hysterically. Harold put a hand on her arm "I say, old girl, steady on" he said. "You're just about all in, you know, the sooner we get you to bed the better".

If only she *could* escape to bed, thought Lois, as she cut a piece of her anchovy egg into smaller and smaller squares at supper that night, if only she could escape from this endless monologue of Daisy's. They really were the two most selfish, thoughtless people she had ever known, if anything Harold was worse than Daisy. He knew what a strain she had been through that day, she had already been at breaking point when they arrived at Miss Wheeler's, but had steeled herself to meet the ordeal of her father's reception. Daddy had been so terribly ill after the slight jolting when he was carried upstairs, at one point fluid seemed to be pouring from every part of his body at once. She had to admit that Miss Wheeler and Dr. Grimmett had been very kind and, what was more important, efficient. But it had been pitiful to see his poor body when they had washed him, and he had cried with the pain, great, heavy sobs. She had never heard him cry before and she had almost broken down. Despite Miss Wheeler's kindness, the whole house seemed so unsuitable, with sounds of babies' yelling and a smell of nappies on the landing. She had sworn an oath that she would rescue him, but meanwhile things were better than she had dared to hope. It was well after nine o'clock before they got back to the house and Daisy had still not returned. She had wanted to go to bed, but Harold had said that Daisy would be so disappointed, had assured her it would only be a question of a few minutes. It was ten o'clock before Daisy came in and they sat down to what she was told was a "scratch meal". Now it was almost eleven and all that time Daisy had been talking and eating continuously—sausage rolls, sardine sandwiches, savoury eggs, rock cakes, anything within reach. Lois had felt too tired to hear most of what her sister-in-law said, so that she had been watching this voracious consumption as though she had been lucky enough to arrive at the Mappin Terrace at 4 p.m. And really, it was exactly like some animal, for Daisy opened her mouth very wide, talking all the time that she was eating, and swallowing enormous mouthfuls, yes, and spitting wet globules of food all over the table, added Lois spitefully.

There seemed to be so much of Daisy, enormous bosom, rows of teeth, wisps of hair that knew no control, huge arms and a voluminous black and white foulard dress with angel sleeves, the ends of which dipped into every dish as she reached across the table. She must have a digestion like an ox to eat all this heavy food so quickly. I know I shall never sleep after what I've eaten, Lois thought.

"Rubbish! Harold" her sister-in-law was saying "the trouble with the City of London is that they haven't got any guts. They're simply putting their own financial interests before the country's good. Anything more shortsighted than their socalled realism, I cannot imagine. A 10 per cent, dividend may be very nice, but it's not much help if we're going to sit by and sink to the position of a second rate power."

"I think you're inclined to misjudge the Government a bit, you know, old dear" said her husband. "There's a point beyond which we shall never concede. But modern war's a nasty business, it's not like the old days of shining armour. You can't go to war over every tinpot European country created at Versailles by a lot of men who didn't know geography. I think we can rest assured Chamberlain's keeping an eye open and if they go too far with us we shall say no".

"And meanwhile we're letting that man take every key point in Europe. Really, Harold, as if I didn't have enough of it all the evening. I'm as loyal a Conservative as anyone, but I hope I shall never put party before country".

"I suppose you'd rather have the Labour Party".

"With peace ballots and unilateral disarmament, no thank you. No, we're the only party who can save the Empire and that's exactly why we've got to pull our socks up. There's too much attachment to individuals that's the trouble. Some of the old guard have done wonderfully well, but they aren't big enough for the situation and if they can't adapt themselves they must go, that's all. Thank God, Mrs. Faulkner tells me her brother in the War Office says the service chiefs have started kicking up a row at last, about time too. Have you heard anything of that, Lois?" she asked.

"I haven't heard about any of it" said Lois. "You see I've been nursing Daddy".

Daisy was taken aback for a moment, then she got up from her seat and put her hand on Lois' shoulder.

"Poor old Lois" she said "too bad, my dear. Never mind we'll be taking the burden on now".

Lois moved away from her "I have been proud to do it". Daisy decided to ignore this remark. "Motion before the house: bed" she said. "Carried unanimously".

When they visited Mr. Gorringe the next morning he showed a remarkable improvement, he was sitting up in bed in a little camel hair jacket, his white hair neatly brushed, even his eyes quite bright. Daisy, too, although she had put off her morning engagements, was bright and cheerful. Whilst Miss Wheeler seemed to Lois to be odiously eupeptic. Everyone seems awfully pleased, thought Lois, except me. Miss Wheeler took her aside to tell her that the change for the better in her father's condition was miraculous. "I really thought last night that he was going to pop off the hooks" she said "but he's wonderfully rested, dear old gentleman. Dr. Grimmett says we'll have him out and about in a wheel chair in next to no time if he goes on like this". Lois could not help wishing that she too could feel "wonderfully rested" as she thought bitterly of the battles she had fought all night in defence of her father, the tears she had wept in anger at the day's events.

"Miss Wheeler and I are famous friends" said Mr. Gorringe. "We've made a bargain—she cuts my beard and I give her the winner of the 2.30".

Miss Wheeler laughed appreciatively and winked across at Daisy. It was just as Harold had promised, she treated Daddy like a child, but somehow Lois had to admit that he did not seem to mind.

"I hear you've made great friends with a little kiddy here" said Daisy.

"It's wonderful" explained Miss Wheeler "the baby took to him at once. She calls him Foonoo". A moment later she came back with the baby in her arms. "Foonoo" she said, pointing at Mr. Gorringe "Foonoo" and "Foonoo" said the baby. Mr. Gorringe laughed delightedly.

"Well, Father" said Daisy, substituting the Schools Programme for the Children's Hour. "What do you think of the mess the country's in?"

"We've got to tell Hitler and Musso where they get off" said Mr. Gorringe. "Good for you, Father" said Daisy "that's what I told the local party yesterday" and "Good for you" said Mr. Gorringe.

A little later Lois managed to get close to her father, while Miss Wheeler and Daisy were busy talking. "Are you sure you're alright, Daddy darling" she said. "You

don't have to stay if you don't like it. *I'll* get you away".
Mr. Gorringe looked puzzled. "Don't you worry your
head, girlie", he said "the old woman's a very decent sort.
You ought to be cutting back to town, you don't want to
upset them at the office". Lois bent down and kissed her
father. "As if the office counted beside you, darling" she
said. But Mr. Gorringe only answered rather impatiently
"I'll be alright, girlie". Then he looked up at the baby in
Miss Wheeler's arms. "That kid's a second Dempsey"
he said "look at those wicked uppercuts with the right".
Suddenly Lois' voice sounded in the room shrill and
shaking "I shall go now" she said "I'll get the next train.
Yes, really I must. Don't bother I can find my way to the
station. I shall be at Marjorie Boothby's for the next few
days, you can find it in the 'phone book if you want me.
Good-bye, darling" and she kissed her father's brow "I'll
come and see you again soon".

Lois was doing her hair and Marjorie was in the bath
when the telephone rang. They were dining in Soho with
the Travises, but they had promised to look in at Mavis
Wayne's party before dinner. "See who it is, darling"
called Marjorie. When Lois lifted the receiver she recognized Daisy's voice. "It's me speaking, Daisy" she said.
"Oh, Lois dear, I rang to tell you father's not so well.
He's had a relapse. It's definite uremia, Doctor Grimmett
says. He's not conscious, in a coma, you know. Harold and
I thought we should tell you; the doctor says he may go at
any time. He's not suffering any pain though, Lois, I know
you'll be glad to hear that. Shall we expect you down?"

"No," said Lois. "It's really only of historical interest"
and she realized suddenly that she was repeating Dr.
Filby's words.

"What did you say, dear? I couldn't hear" Daisy sounded puzzled.

"I said there doesn't seem to be much point in my coming down if he's in a coma" said Lois. "You'll let me know if he asks for me, of course".

"Of course" repeated Daisy and she still sounded puzzled.

"Well, good-bye" said Lois and she put down the receiver. "Are you nearly ready, Marjorie?" she called. "Will there be hundreds of interesting, new people? I'm rather in the mood to meet hundreds of interesting, new people".

The Wrong Set

JUST before the club closed, Mrs. Lippiatt asked very specially for a medley of old numbers. Mr. Pontresoli himself came over and told Terry. "It's for your bundle of charms" he said "so don't blame me". Vi wanted to refuse when Terry asked her—she had a filthy headache and anyway she was sick of being kept late. "Tell the old cow to go and . . ." she was saying, when Terry put a finger on her lips. "Do it for me, dear" he said. "Remember without her I don't eat". Poor Kid! thought Vi, having to do it with an old trout like that, old enough to be his grandmother—still she stank of money, he was on to a good thing if he could keep it. So she put on a special sweet smile and waved at Mrs. Lippiatt. "Here's wishing you all you wish yourself, dear" she called. Then she smiled at Mr. Pontresoli, just to show him how hard she worked for his lousy club—might as well kill two birds with one stone. "Let it go, Terry" she called and the two pianos jazzed out the old duet routine—Souvenirs, Paper Doll, Some of these Days, Blue Again, everything nice and corney. It was while they were playing "The Sheik of Araby" that she noticed Mrs. Lippiatt's face—all lit up with memories. Christ! she must be old if she goes back to that, thought Vi, and then she said to herself "Poor old bitch, she must have been pretty once, but, there you are, that's life, makes you hard". At least she'd got a nice bit of stuff in Terry, best looking boy in the place; not that she didn't prefer something a bit nearer her own age herself, and she gazed proudly over at Trevor, with his wavy grey hair and soldier's moustache, talking to Mr.

Pontresoli. Funny how class told. Old Pontresoli could have bought Trevor up any day, but there he was, respectful as anything, listening to what Trevor had to say. She could hear Trevor's voice above the music "My dear old Ponto, you'll never change that sort of thing in this country till you clear out the Yids". If Mr. Pontresoli knew what Trevor really thought of him! "Filthy wop" he'd said, but he'd agreed to be nice, because of Vi's piano act and until he got a job they needed all the money she could earn.

After closing time she had a drink with Terry and Mrs. Lippiatt. Mrs. Lippiatt said what was the good of having money, there was nothing to spend it on. Vi thought to herself what she would like was to have some money to spend, but aloud she said in her smart voice "Yes, isn't it awful? With this government you have to be grateful for the air you breathe. Look at the things we can't have— food, clothes, foreign travel". "Ah, yes, foreign travel" said Mrs. Lippiatt, though she knew damned well Vi had never been abroad. "It's bad enough for you and me, Mrs. Cawston, but think of this poor boy"and she put her fat, beringed hand on Terry's knee *"he's* never been out of England. Never mind, darling, you shall have your trip to Nice the day we get a proper government back". Mr. Pontresoli and Trevor joined them. Trevor was the real public schoolboy with his monocle and calling Mrs. Lippiatt "my dear lady", Vi could see that Terry was worried—he was frightened that Trevor was muscling in; but that was just Trevor's natural way with women— he had perfect manners. Later in the evening he asked Vi who the hell the old trout was.

"The Major's got a good one about Attlee" said Mr. Pontresoli in his thick, adenoidal Italian cockney, his series of blue stubbed chins wobbling as he spoke.

G

"It's impossible to be as funny about this government as they are themselves" said Trevor. He had *such* a quiet sense of humour. "They're a regular Fred Karno show". But they all begged to hear the story, so he gave it to them. "An empty taxi drove up to No. 10", he said "and Mr. Attlee got out". Beautifully told it was, with his monocle taken out of his eye and polished just at the right moment.

"Well Sir Stafford gives me the creeps" said Terry. No one thought that very funny except Mrs. Lippiatt and she roared.

"Are you ready, young woman?" Trevor said to Vi with mock severity "because I'm not waiting all night". As she was coming out of the ladies', Vi met Mona and her girl friend. She stopped and talked to them for a minute although she knew Trevor would disapprove. It was true, of course, that that sort of thing was on the increase and Trevor said it was the ruin of England, but then he said that about so many things—Jews and foreigners, the Labour Government and the Ballet. Anyhow Mona's crowd had been very kind to her in the old days when she was down to her last sausage, and when they'd found she wasn't their sort there'd never been so much as a word to upset her.

"For Christ's sake, Kiddie" said Trevor "I wish you wouldn't talk to those Lizzies".

On the stairs they met young Mr. Solomons. Vi *had* to talk to him, whatever Trevor said. First of all he was important at the club, and then his smile always got her—nice and warm somehow like a cat purring, but that was what she felt about a lot of Jews. "She's stood me up, Vi" he said, his eyes round with pretended dismay "left me in the lurch. Ah! I ought to have stuck to nice girls like you". Vi couldn't help laughing, but Trevor was wild with anger. He stood quite still for a moment in Denman Street under the electric sign which read "Passion Fruit Club". "If I catch that lousy Yid hanging around you again, girlie", he said "I'll knock his ruddy block off". All the way in the tube to Earls Court he was in a rage. Vi wanted to tell him that she was going to visit her nephew Norman tomorrow, but she feared his reception of the news. Trevor had talked big about helping Norman, when she told him the boy had won a scholarship at London University and was coming to live with them. But somehow her sister Ivy had got word that she wasn't really married to Trevor and they'd sent the boy elsewhere. She and Trevor had taken him out to dinner once in the West End—a funny boy with tousled black hair and thick spectacles who never said a word, though he'd eaten a hearty enough meal and laughed fit to split at the Palladium. Trevor said he wasn't all there and the less they saw of him the better, but Vi thought of him as her only relative in London and after all Ivy *was* her sister, even if she was so narrow.

"I'm going to see Norman tomorrow" Vi said timidly, as they crossed the Earls Court Road.

"Good God" cried Trevor "What on earth for, girlie?"

"I've written once or twice to that Hampstead address and had no reply".

"Well, let the little swine stew in his own juice if he hasn't the decency to answer" said Trevor.

"Blood's blood after all" countered Vi, and so they argued until they were back in their bed-sitting room. Vi put on a kimono and feathered mules, washed off her make-up and covered her face in cream until it shone with highlights. Then she sat plucking her eyebrows. Trevor put his trousers to press under the mattress, gave himself a whisky in the toothglass, refilled it with Milton and water

and put in his dentures. Then he sat in his pants, sus-
penders and socks squeezing blackheads from his nose in
front of a mirror. All this time they kept on rowing. At
last Vi cried out "Alright, alright, Trevor Cawston, but
I'm *still* going". "O.K." said Trevor "how's about a
little loving?" So then they broke into the old routine.

When the time came to visit Norman, Vi was in quite a
quandary about what to wear. She didn't want the people
he lived with to put her down as tarty—there'd probably
been quite enough of that sort of talk already—on the
other hand she wasn't going to look a frump for anyone.
She compromised with her black suit, white lace jabot
and gold pocket seal, with coral nail varnish instead of
scarlet.

The house when she got there wasn't in Hampstead at
all, but in Kilburn. Respectable, she decided, but a bit
poor looking.

"Norman's out at the demo." said Mrs. Thursby "but
he should be back any time now. You'll come in and have
a cup of tea, won't you?" Vi said she thought she would.
She hadn't quite understood where her nephew was, but if
he was coming back soon, she might as well wait. The
parlour into which she was ushered brought her home in
Leicester back to her—all that plush, and the tassels and
the china with crests on it got her down properly now.
One thing they wouldn't have had at home though and
that was all those books, cases full of them, and stacks of
newspapers and magazines piled on the floor, and then
there was a typewriter—probably a studious home, she
decided. She did wish the little dowdy, bright-eyed woman
with the bobbed hair would sit down instead of hopping
about like a bird. But Mrs. Thursby had heard something

about Vi, and she was at once nervous and hostile; she stood making little plucking gestures at her necklace and her sleeve ends and shooting staccato inquiries at Vi in a chirping voice that had an undertone of sarcasm.

"Mrs. . . . Mrs. Cawston, is it?"

"That's right" said Vi.

"Oh yes. I wasn't quite sure. It's so difficult to know sometimes these days, isn't it? with . . . ." and Mrs. Thursby's voice trailed away.

Vi felt she was being got at. But Mrs. Thursby went on talking.

"Oh! The man *will* be sorry you came when he was out". By calling Norman "The man" she seemed to be claiming a greater relationship to him than that of a mere aunt. "He's talked of you" and she paused, then added drily "a certain amount. I won't say a great deal, but then he's not a great talker".

"Where did you say he was?" asked Vi.

"At Trafalgar Square" said Mrs. Thursby. "They're rallying there to hear Pollitt or one of those people. My two went, they're both C.P., and Norman's gone with them. Though I'm glad to say he's had the good sense not to join up completely, he's just a fellow traveller as they call them."

Vi was too bemused to say much, but she managed to ask for what purpose they were rallying.

"To make trouble for the Government they put into power" said Mrs. Thursby drily. "It makes me very angry sometimes. It's taken us forty years to get a real Labour Government and then just because they don't move fast enough for these young people, it's criticism, criticism all the time. But, there it is, I've always said the same, there's no fool like a young fool" and she closed her tight, little mouth with relish "they'll come round in time. Hilda, that's my girl, was just the same about the chapel, but now it seems they've agreed to the worship of God. Very kind of them I'm sure. I expect you feel the same as I do, Mrs. Cawston".

Vi wasn't quite sure exactly what Mrs. Thursby did feel, but she *was* sure that she didn't agree, so she said defiantly "I'm conservative".

"Lena" said Mrs. Thursby in a dry, abrupt voice to a tall, middle-aged woman who was bringing in the tea-tray "We've got a Tory in the house. The first for many a day".

"Oh no!" said Lena, and everything about her was charming and gemütlich from her foreign accent to her smile of welcome. "I am so pleased to meet you but it is terrible that you are a Tory".

"Miss Untermayer teaches the man German" said Mrs. Thursby. "Mrs. Cawston is Norman's aunt."

"Oh!" cried Miss Untermayer, her gaunt features lit up with almost girlish pleasure "Then I congratulate you. You have a very clever nephew".

Vi said she was sure she was pleased to hear that, but she didn't quite like the sound of these rallies.

"Oh! that" said Miss Untermayer "He will grow out of that. All this processions and violence, it is for children. But Norman is a very spiritual boy, I am sure that he is a true pacifist."

"I'm sure I hope not" said Vi who was getting really angry. "I've never had anything to do with conchies."

"Then you've missed contact with a very fine body of men" said Mrs. Thursby "Mr. Thursby was an objector".

"I'm sorry, I'm sure" said Vi. "Major Cawston was right through the war."

"The important thing is that he came out the other side" remarked Mrs. Thursby drily.

"There are so many kinds of bravery, so many kinds of courage. I think we must respect them all". Miss Untermayer's years as a refugee had made her an adept at glossing over divisions of opinion. All the same she gave a sigh of relief when Norman's voice was heard in the hall, at least the responsibility would not be on *her* any more.

"Hilda and Jack have gone on to a meeting" he shouted "I'd have gone too but I've got to get on with this essay".

"You aunt's come to see you" shouted back Mrs. Thursby.

Norman came into the room sideways like a crab, he was overcome with confusion at the sight of Vi and he stood, running his hands through his hair and blinking behind his spectacles.

"You were such a long time answering my letters that I thought I'd better come down and see what sort of mischief you'd got into" said Vi "and I have" she added bitterly. "Demonstrations indeed. I'd like to know what your mother would say, Norman Hackett?"

Norman's face was scarlet as he looked up, but he answered firmly. "I don't think Mum would disapprove, not if she understood. And even if she did, it couldn't make any difference."

"Not make any difference what your mother said. I'm ashamed of you, Norman, mixing up with a lot of reds and Jews".

"That's enough of that" cried Mrs. Thursby. "We'll not have any talk against Jews in this house. No, not even from Rahab herself."

Vi's face flushed purple underneath her makeup. "You ought to be ashamed" she cried "an old woman like you to let a boy of Norman's age mix up with all this trash."

"You've no right to say that. . . ." began Norman, but Mrs. Thursby interrupted him. "Oh let the woman say her say, Norman. I've had a windful of Tory talk before now and it hasn't killed me. If Father and I have taught the man to stand up for his own class, we're proud of it. And now, Mrs. Cawston, if you've nothing more to say to Norman, I think you'd better go."

Vi arrived at the Unicorn sharp at opening time that evening. She'd got over most of her indignation, after all Ivy didn't think much about *her*, and if the boy wanted to go to pot, good riddance. She had a couple of gins and lime as she waited for Trevor.

Mr. Pontresoli came across the saloon bar. "Hullo, Vi" he said in his thick voice "Have you heard the news about Solomons? Dreadful, isn't it?"

It really gave Vi quite a shock to hear that they'd charged young Mr. Solomons—something to do with clothing coupons. She had felt quite guilty towards him after speaking out like that against the Jews, and now to hear of this, it made you wonder what sort of a government we *had* got. As Mr. Pontresoli said "It's getting to be the end of liberty, you mark my words".

"Trevor'll have something to say about this, Mr. Pontresoli" Vi said, and then she remembered what Trevor said about the Jews, it was all too difficult, one could never tell. Mr. Pontresoli offered her another gin, so she said yes. "I'll tell you what" said Mr. Pontresoli "It's going to make a difference to me financially. Solomons was one of my best backers at the club. It may mean cutting down a bit. We shan't be needing two pianos."

What with the gin—will you have another? said Mr.

Pontresoli, and yes said Vi—and the tiring day she'd had, Vi felt quite cast down as she thought of Terry out of a job. A nice boy like that. But then he'd got Mrs. Lippiatt.

"Poor Terry, Mr. Pontresoli" she said, her eyes filling with tears "We *shall* miss him at the club. Here's wishing him more Mrs. Lippiatts" and she drained her glass. "This one's on me, Mr. Pontresoli" she said, and Mr. Pontresoli agreed.

"We couldn't afford to let Terry go" said Mr. Pontresoli "that's certain. Mrs. Lippiatt says he draws all the women, and she ought to know, she spends so much money".

Vi worked all this out and it seemed to come round to her. This made her angry. "Why that's nonsense, Mr. Pontresoli" she said, and she smiled broadmindedly "surely you know Terry's a pansy".

Mr. Pontresoli's fat, cheerful, face only winked. "That gets 'em all ways" he said and walked out of the saloon bar.

Vi felt quite desperate. She couldn't think where Trevor had got to. "Have you seen my husband Major Cawston, Gertie?" she asked the barmaid. No one could say I haven't got dignity when I want it, she thought. Gertie hadn't seen Trevor, but Mona's girl friend said she had, twenty minutes ago at the George *and* stinking. No job and Trevor stinking. It all made Vi feel very low. Life was hell anyhow, and with all those Reds, she'd go after Trevor and fetch Norman back. She was about to get down from the high stool, when she noticed that Mona's girl friend's eyes were red. "What's the matter, dear?" she asked.

"Mona's gone off with that Bretonne bitch" said the girl. "Oh dear" said Vi solemnly "That's very bad". So they both had another drink to help them on. Vi was in battling mood. "Go out and fetch Mona back" she cried. "You won't get anywhere sitting still". "You do talk silly sometimes" said the girl "What can I do against a Bretonne, they're so passionate".

The sadness of it all overcame Vi, it was all so true and so sad and so true—all those Bretonnes and Reds and passionates, and Trevor going off to demos, no, Norman going off to demos, and Mr. Solomons in the hands of the Government, and her nephew in the hands of the Reds. Yes, that was the chief thing.

"I must let my sister know that her son's in trouble" she said. "How can I tell her?"

"Ring her up" suggested Mona's friend, but Vi told her Ivy had no 'phone. "Send a telegram, dear, that's what I should do" said Gertie. "You can use the 'phone at the back of the bar. Just dial TEL."

It took Vi some time to get through to Telegrams, the telephone at the Unicorn seemed to be such a difficult one. I mustn't let Ivy know that I'm in this condition, she thought, she was always the grand lady with Ivy, so holding herself erect and drawling slightly, she said "I want to send a telegram to my sister, please. The name is Hackett—44 Guybourne Road, Leicester. Terribly worried". It sounded very Mayfair and she repeated it "Terribly worried. Norman in the Wrong Set. Vi." "I feel much better now, Gertie" she said as she stumbled back to the bar. "I've done my duty".

Crazy Crowd

JENNIE leaned forward and touched him on the knee. "What are you thinking about, darling?" she asked. "I was thinking about Tuesday" Peter said. "It was nice, wasn't it?" said Jennie, and for a moment the memory of being in bed with him filled her so completely that she lay back with her eyes closed and her lips slightly apart. This greatly excited Peter and he felt the presence of the old gentleman in the opposite corner of the carriage as an intolerable intrusion. A moment later she was staring at him, her large dark eyes with their long lashes dwelling on him with that sincere, courageous look that made him worship her so completely. "All the same, Peter, I wish you didn't have to say Tuesday in that special voice". "What should I have said?" he asked nervously. "I should have thought you could have said 'I was thinking how nice it was when we were in bed together' or something like that". Peter laughed "I see what you mean" he said. "I wonder if you do". "I think so. You prefer to call a spade a spade". "No, I don't" said Jennie. "Spades have nothing to do with it" she lit a cigarette with an abrupt, angry gesture. "There's nothing shocking about it. No unpleasant facts to be faced. It's just that I don't like covering over something rather good and pleasant with all that stickiness, that hesitating and making it sacred with a special kind of hushed voice. I think that kind of thing clogs up the works". "Yes" said Peter "Perhaps it does. But isn't it just a convention? Does it mean any more?" "I think so" said Jennie "I think it does". She put on her amber rimmed glasses and took out her Hugo's Italian Course. Peter felt completely sick; he must make it alright with her now or there would be one of those angry silences that he could not bear. "I do understand what you mean" he said "I just didn't get it for a moment that was all". Jennie wrinkled up her nose at him and pressed his hand softly. "Never mind, silly" she said and smiled, but she went back to her Italian grammar.

Peter longed to say something more, to make sure that everything was all right, but he remembered what Jennie had said to him about wasting time trying to undo things that were done. As he looked at her peering so solemnly at the book in front of her and making notes on a piece of paper from time to time, he felt once more how privileged he was to have won her love. She was so clear-sighted, so firm in her judgments, so tenacious in her application. Here she was learning Italian, and learning it competently, not just playing at it, and all because she intended a visit to Italy some time next year. They had almost quarrelled about it some weeks ago when she had refused to go to Studio One to see the Raimu film because she had her next lesson to prepare. "Aren't you being rather goody-goody about all this?" he had said, but she had shown him immediately how false was his perspective. "No, darling, it's not a question of being good, it's just a matter of thinking ahead a little, being sensible even if it means being a bore sometimes. If I went to Italy without having read something of their literature and without being able to speak adequately I should feel such a fraud". "You mean because you would be having something on easy terms that others could appreciate more". "No, no" she had cried "damn all that about others, that's just sentimentality. No, I'm thinking of myself, of my own integrity. Peter, surely you can see that one must have some clear picture of one's life in front of one. You can't just grab at pleasure like a greedy schoolboy, Raimu this evening because I want it, no Italian because I don't. The whole thing would be such an impossible mess". Then she had leaned over the back of his chair and stroked his hair. "Listen to me" she had said "talking to you like this, you who have done so much with your life even at twenty-seven, fighting that dismal Baptist background, winning scholarships, getting a First, being an officer in His Majesty's Navy and now being an A.P. at the Ministry and a jolly good A.P. too. That's really the trouble, you've read everything, you know all the languages, I don't. Be patient with me, darling, be patient with my ignorance". She had paused for a moment, frowning, then she had added "Not that I think you should ever stop learning. The trouble is, you know, that you've got swallowed up by the Ministry. Town planning is a wonderful thing but it isn't enough for someone like you, you need something creative in your leisure time too".

Of course he realized that she was right, he had fallen into the habit of thinking that he could rest on his laurels. There had been so much activity in the past few years, constant examinations, adapting himself to new situations, new strata of society, first Cambridge, then the Navy, and now the Ministry and life in London, he had begun to think that he could rest for a bit and just have fun, provided he did his job properly. But Jennie had seen through that. It wasn't as if she could not have fun too when she wanted it, and in a far more abandoned, less inhibited way than he could ever manage, but she had a sense of balance, had not been thrown out of gear by the war. And so he had promised to resume his University research work on the Pléiade.

Peter opened the new book on Du Bellay and read a few pages, but somehow with Jennie sitting opposite he could not concentrate and he began to stare out of the window. Already the train was moving through the flats of Cambridgeshire: an even yellow surface of grass after the summer's heat, cut by the crisscross of streams with their thick rushes and pollarded willows; only occasionally did the eye find a focal point—the hard black and white of some Frisians pasturing, the rusty symmetry of a Georgian mansion, the golden billowing of a copse in the September wind, and—marks of creeping urbanization—the wire fences and outhouses of the smallholdings with their shining white geese and goats. It seemed strange to think that Jennie's home which she had painted in such warm, happy, even, if the word had not been debased, cosy colours should lie among such plain, almost deadening landscape. But as Peter gazed longer he began to feel that there was a dependability, an honest good sense about these levels that was much what he admired so in her, and perhaps as she had built that brilliant, gay attractive nature upon plain and good foundation, so the Cockshotts had created their home alive, bright, happy go lucky, "crazy", Jennie had often described it, upon this sensible land.

He tried to picture her family from the many things she had said about them. His own home background was so different that he found it difficult to follow her warm, impulsive description of her childhood. Respect for parents, he understood, and acceptance of the recognized forms and ceremonies or else rebellion from them, but he had been far too busy winning scholarships and passing examinations to attempt the intimate undertones, the almost emotional companionship of which Jennie spoke, nor would his parents, with their austere conceptions of filial obedience tempered only by their ambitions for his future, have understood or encouraged such overtures. He felt greatly drawn to the easy familiarity that she had described, yet much afraid that her family would not like him.

It was clear that the only course was to maintain a friendly silence and trust to Jennie to interpret as she had done so often in London. Her affection for her father was deep and he imagined it was reciprocated. Indeed the wealthy barrister who had retired from the law so early sounded a most attractive gentle creature, with his love of the country, his local antiquarianism and his great artistic integrity which had caused him to publish so little, to polish and polish as he aimed at perfection. A survival, of course, but a lovable and amusing person; Peter's only fear was that he would fail to grasp the many leisured-class hypotheses by which Mr. Cockshott obviously lived, but there again Jennie had explained so much.

Her stepmother, Nan, remained more vague. Some children, certainly, would have resented the intrusion of an American woman into their home, but Jennie and her brother had apparently completely accepted Nan, though there were clearly things in her that Jennie felt difficult to assimilate, for she often said laughingly that her stepmother had on such and such an occasion been "rather pathetically Yankee". Thinking of the garrulous, over-earnest American academical women he had known, Peter had thought this an unpleasant condemnation; but his acquaintance was very limited, and Jennie had explained that Southerners were quite different "awfully English really, only with an extra chic for which any English girl would sell her all". Peter thought that perhaps Nan might be a little alarming, but obviously very worth while.

Then there was Jennie's brother Hamish who had been her companion in all those strange, happy fantasy games of her childhood. She had explained carefully that he was not an intellectual, but that he was very learned in country lore and had read all sorts of out of the way books on subjects that interested him. Jennie admired him because he had hammered out ideas for himself in so many different spheres—had his own philosophy of life and his own views on art and politics. Some of these views sounded strangely crazy to Peter, and perhaps a bit cock-sure, but still he was only twenty-two and as Jennie had pointed out views didn't matter when one was young, what really counted was thinking for oneself. It would be necessary to go very easy with a fellow like that, Peter reflected, thinking of his own obstinate defence of heterodox ideas at that age: it had been mostly due to shyness he remembered. And lastly there was Flopsy, who was some sort of cousin, though he could never un-ravel the exact relationship. She was certainly somebody outside his former experience, not that he was unused to the presence of elderly unmarried female relations in the homes of family friends, but their activities were always confined to household matters, women's gossip or good works. This Flopsy was a much more positive character, for not only did she run the household, and with such a happy go lucky family she must be kept very busy, but she appeared also to be the confidante of all their troubles. The extent to which even someone so self reliant as Jennie depended upon her advice was amazing, but she was obviously a rare sort of person. He felt that he already knew and liked her from the many stories he had heard of her downright tongue, her great commonsense and her sudden frivolities, he only hoped that he would not fall too much below her idea of the ideal suitor, but at least he felt that so shrewd and honest a woman would see through his awkwardness to his deep love for Jennie. Anyhow, he decided, if anything went wrong it would only be his own fault, for it was really a privilege to be meeting such unusual people who were yet so simple and warm hearted, above all it was a great privilege to be meeting Jennie's family.

As she stepped from the carriage on to the little country platform Jennie looked back for a moment at her lover. "Frightened, darling?" she asked and as Peter nodded assent "There's no earthly need" she said "I'm pretty certain you'll approve of them and I know they'll love you. Anyhow anyone who fails to make the grade will have to reckon with me. So you've been warned" she ended with mock severity. A sudden gust of wind blew from behind her as she stood on the platform, causing her to hold tightly to the little red straw hat perched precariously on her head, blowing the thick, dark wavy hair in strands on which the sun played, moulding her cherry and white flowered dress to her slender figure, underlining the beauty of her long, well-shaped legs. It gave a moment's sharp desire to Peter that made him fear the discomfort of the weekend, doubt his ability to keep their mutual bond that parental feelings were to be respected, lovemaking foresworn.

But desire could not endure, already they had been claimed by Nan. "Honey" she cried in her soft Southern drawl, throwing her arms round Jennie's neck "Honey, it's good to see you. I know it's only a week, but it's seemed like an age". "Darling Nan" cried Jennie, and her embrace was almost that of a little girl, as she kicked her feet up behind her. "Darling Nan, this is Peter. Peter, this is Nan". The sunburnt, florid face, with its upturned, freckled nose turned to Peter, the blue eyes gazed steadily

H

at him, then Nan broke into a broad, goodnatured smile, the wide, loose mouth parting to reveal even, white teeth. She gave Peter's hand a hearty shake "My! this is a good moment" she said. "A very good moment". Then she turned again to Jennie, and holding her at arm's length. "You look awfully pale, dear" she said "I hate to think of you up there in those dreadful smoky streets, and it's been so lovely here. We have the most beautiful autumns here, Peter". "They're the same as autumns anywhere else, darling" said Jennie. "That they're not" said Nan "Everything's kind of special round here. You just wait till you see our trees, Peter, great splendid red and gold creatures. I better warn you I shan't like you at all if you don't fall in love with our countryside. But I know you will, you're no townsman, not with those powerful shoulders. I like your Peter" she said to Jennie. "There you are, darling, she likes you". "Well, for heaven's sake, look at that" cried Nan "Hamish hasn't moved out of the car" and she pointed at a tall, dark-haired young man whose legs seemed to fill the back of the grey car towards which they were advancing.

It gave Peter a shock to see Jennie's eyes staring from a man's face. He felt the moment had come to be positive. "Hullo, Hamish" he said with what he hoped was a friendly smile, but the young man ignored him. "That's a revolting dress" he said to Jennie, in a mumble that came from behind his pipe. "Not so revolting as a green tie with a blue shirt" said his sister. "Really, darling, you need me here to take your colour sense in hand". "Parkinson's wife been took again, and it's a mercy she come through, what with being her eighth and born with a hump like a camel" said Hamish. "Never" said Jennie "and her such a good woman. What be they callin' 'the littl'un?'" "They don't give 'er no name" said Hamish "for fear she be bewitched". "'Appen it'll be so" said Jennie.

"For heaven's sake, you two" said Nan "What will Peter think of you? Aren't they the craziest pair? Look at poor Peter standing there wondering what sort of place he's come to". Peter endeavoured to explain that he understood them to be imitating rustics, but Nan would not allow him to comprehend. "My dear, there's no need to hide it from me. I know exactly what you're thinking 'What ever made me come down to this crazy place among these crazy people?' And so they are—the crazy Cockshotts. My dear" she called to Jennie in the back of the car "it's going to be the most terrible picnic, I've just not thought a thing about what to eat or what to drink, so Heaven knows what you'll find, children". "Never mind, darling," called Jennie "the Lord will provide". "He'd better" said Nan "or I'll never go to that awful old church again".

To Peter sitting in front with her it seemed that Nan never ceased speaking for the whole nine miles of their drive to the house. He could not help feeling that in her garrulity she was much like other American women, but he felt sure that he was missing some quality through his own obtuseness. He found it easy enough to answer her innumerable questions for a murmur of assent was all she required; her sudden changes, however, from talk about the village and rationing or praise of the countryside to a more intimate note confused him greatly. "I do hope you're going to like us" she said, fixing him with her honest blue eyes, to the great detriment of her driving "because I know we're going to like you very, very much".

As a background to Nan's slow drawl he could hear a constant conversation in varying degrees of rustic accent, coming from the back of the car, sometimes giving place to giggles from Jennie and great guffaws from Hamish, sometimes to horseplay in which wrestling and hair pulling were followed by shrieks of laughter. Only twice did the two conversations merge. "Jennie" called Nan once "You never told me Peter was a beautiful young man. He's beautiful". "Nan, Nan, don't say it. You'll make him conceited" said Jennie. "I can't help it" said Nan "If I see anything beautiful, whether it's trees or flowers or a lovely physique I just have to say so". "He's certainly better than Jennie's last young man" said Hamish "the one with spavins and a cauliflower ear. Peter's ears appear to be of the normal size". "We pride ourselves on our ears in my family" said Peter, trying to join in the fun, but Hamish was intent on his own act. "Then there was the young dental mechanic, a charming fellow, indeed brilliant as dental mechanics go, but unfortunately he smelt. You don't smell, do you?" he called to Peter. "Don't be rude, Hamish" said Jennie, and Nan chimed in with "Now Hamish you're just being horrible and coarse". "Ah, I forgot" said Hamish "the susceptibilities of the great bourgeoisie, no reference must ever be made to the effects of the humours of the human body upon the olfactory nerves. Peter, I apologize".

Luckily Peter was not called upon to reply, for Nan directed his attention to a Queen Anne house. "My! what a shame" she said "the Piggotts are from home. I know you'd just adore the Piggotts. They're the most wonderful, old English family. They've lived in that lovely old house for generations, but to meet them they're the simplest folk imaginable. Why! old Sir Charles looks just like a dear old farmer. . . ." and she continued happily to discourse on the necessary interdependence of good breeding and simplicity, occasionally adding remarks to the effect that having roots deep in the countryside was what really mattered. Suddenly she paused and shouting over her shoulder to Jennie she called "My dear the most awful thing! I quite forgot to tell you we've all got to go to the Bogush-Smiths to tea". "Oh, Nan, no!" cried Jennie "not the Bogus-S's". "We always call them the Bogus-Smiths" said Nan by way of explanation "they're a terrible vulgar family that comes from Heaven knows where. They've got the most lovely old place, a darling old eighteenth century dower house, but they've just ruined it. They've made it all olde-worlde, of course they just haven't got any taste. Don't you agree, Peter, that vulgarity is the most dreadful of the Deadly Sins?" Peter murmured assent. "I knew you would" said Nan "I wish you could see Mrs. Bogush-Smith gardening in all her rings. I just hate to see hands in a garden when they don't really belong to the soil. The awful thing is, Jennie" she added "that everything grows there. I suppose" she ended with a sigh "people just have green fingers or they haven't". "The Bogus-S's have *money*" said Hamish "and a sense of the power of money, that's what I like about them. If the people who really belong to the land are effete and weak and humane, then let those who have money and are prepared to use it ruthlessly take over. I can respect the Bogus-Smiths' vulgarity, it's strong. When I'm with them it's gloves off. Mr. Bogus-S. sweats his workmen and Mrs. Bogus-S. her servants but they've got what they want. I like going there, it's a clash of wills, my power against theirs". "Hamish is crazy on Power" said Nan explaining again. "Very well, darling you shall go and Peter and Jennie can stay at home. The Brashers will be there". "Oh, hell" said Hamish, and Jennie roaring with laughter began to chant

> *"In their own eyes the Brashers*
> *Are all of them dashers*
> *The Boys are all Mashers*
> *And the girls are all smashers".*

A chorus in which Hamish joined with a deafening roar, and even Nan hummed the tune. "The Brashers shall serve my will and that of the Bogus-Smiths" said Hamish "They shall be our helots". "Thus spake Zarathustra" said Jennie with mock gravity. Hamish began to pull her hat off, and had they not turned into the drive at that moment there would have been another wrestling bout.

They approached a long grey early Victorian house with a verandah and a row of elegant French windows with olive green shutters. "Now isn't it just the ugliest house you've ever seen?" asked Nan. Peter thought it had great charm and said so. "Well, yes" said Nan "the children love it and I suppose it is quaint. But think if it was one of those lovely old red brick Queen Anne farmhouses". A bent old man in a straw hat was tending a chrysanthemum bed, Jennie began to shout excitedly through the window. "Mr. Porpentine, darling Mr. Porpentine" she cried. "What a curious name" said Peter, whose mind had indeed begun to wander under the impact of Nan's chatter. "Oh, Peter, darling, really" said Jennie "It isn't his real name, it's because he's so prickly, you know 'the fretful porpentine'. Only of course he isn't really prickly, he's an old darling". Further explanations were cut short by their arrival at the front porch. Nan led the way into a long, high ceilinged room, into which the sunlight was streaming through the long windows. "This is the sitting room" said Nan "it's in the most terrible mess. But at least it *is* human, it's lived in". And lived in it clearly was—to an unfamiliar visitor like Peter the room appeared like a chart of some crowded group of islands, deep armchairs and sofas in a faded flowered cretonne stood but a few feet from each other, and where the bewildered navigator might hope to pass between them there was always some table or stool to bar his way. Movement was made the more dangerous because some breakable object was balanced precariously on every available flat surface. There were used plates and unused plates, half finished dishes of sandwiches, half empty cups of coffee, ashtrays standing days deep in cigarette ends; even the family photographs on the mantelpiece seemed to be pushing half finished glasses of beer over the edge. It was impossible to sit down, for the chairs and sofas were filled with books, sewing, work-boxes, unfolded newspapers and in one case a tabby cat and two pairs of plyers. When at last some spaces were cleared the chair springs groaned and creaked beneath the weight of their sitters. Peter sank into a chair of which the springs were broken, hitting the calves of his legs against an unsuspected wooden edge. It was clear that the chairs and sofas were each the favourite of some member of the family, had indeed been over long lived in.

"My dears" said Nan "I'm ashamed" and she waved her hand towards a plate of unfinished veal and ham pie that was placed on the "poof". "Suicide Sal's away and we've been picnicking". "Oh I'm so disappointed" cried Jennie "I had so wanted Peter to see Suicide Sal". "My dear, she's had another accident". "T'is Jim Tomlin 'ave got'er into trouble this time" said Hamish. "They do say she be minded to throw 'erself in pond". "Oh! Hamish don't be so dreadful" said Nan and she began to repeat the story of her servant problems that Peter had heard in the car.

Suddenly the door opened and a little birdlike elderly

woman in a neat grey skirt and coat seemed almost to hop into the room. She had a face of faded prettiness with kitten eyes, but at this moment her lips were compressed, her forehead wrinkled, and she was pushing back a wisp of grey hair with a worried gesture. "Oh Nan there you are at last" she said "I just can't get that lemon meringue pie of yours right. The oven won't come down and I'm sure the wretched thing will burn". "Flopsy" cried Jennie and "How's my canary bird?" said Flopsy as they embraced. "Flopsy this is Peter". "How do you do?" said Flopsy "You're taller than I expected and thinner. That young man of yours needs feeding, Jennie. Well, Peter or no Peter he won't get any dinner to-night if we don't look after that pie. Come on Nan". "Happy, darling?" asked Jennie. Peter was too exhausted to do more than smile, but alone with her he felt he could do so sincerely. "Good" she said, then "Where can Daddy be?" she asked and began to call "Dads, Dads, where are you?"

Mr. Cockshott was a much smaller man than Peter had expected. Despite his bald head fringed with grey and his grey toothbrush moustache he had a boyish, almost Puckish expression which made him seem younger than his fifty-seven years. He wore an old, shapeless tweed suit with bulging pockets and a neat grey foulard bow tie. "Jennie, darling, you're looking very pretty" he said, kissing her on the forehead, as she sat on the sofa, and running his hand over her hair. "Dads" said Jennie "darling Dads. This is Peter". "So you're the brave man who's had the temerity to take on this little wretch" said Mr. Cockshott. "It doesn't require much courage" said Peter "the reward is so great". "Good, good" said Mr. Cockshott absently "How are things at the Ministry? Humming, I suppose". It was the first question about

himself that anyone had asked Peter and he was about to
answer when Mr. Cockshoot went on. "Of course they
are. I never yet heard of a Government Office where
things were *not* humming. Though what they're humming about is rather a different question, eh? Well,
you'll find things very quiet down here. Not but what
there's not been a deal of trouble about Abbot Gladwin's
yearly returns. These mortmain tenures are liable to
cause a rumpus you know" he said turning to Jennie.
"It's not like a simple scutage where the return is a plain
per capitem. Between you and me the abbot's had a lot of
trouble with his *own* tenants. I'm by no means sure that
Dame Alice hasn't suppressed a pig or two and as for
Richard the Smith, frankly the man's a liar". "Darling
don't·mystify Peter. He's talking about his old twelfth
century, Peter. Have you had a reply from the Record
Office yet, darling?" "Yes", said Mr. Cockshott "Most
unsatisfactory. Of course it was a turbulent century,
Barrett" he said to Peter "and the turbulence was not
without repercussions even in our remote part of the
world. For instance I've been able to relate the impact of
Richard Coeur de Lion's ransom directly to. . . ." But
there he was interrupted by the return of Nan. "For
heaven's sake, Gordon" she said "just look at you. You
dreadful, disreputable creature. I appeal to you Peter,
doesn't he look just like the wrong end of a salvage
campaign? I just can't imagine what that starchy Mrs.
Brasher will say if she sees you". "If Mrs. Brasher does
see me, and considering her myopic tendencies I consider
that very unlikely, she will undoubtedly, as the current
phrase goes, fall for me". "May be, dear, may be" said
Nan "but nevertheless your trousers are going to get a
patch in them. Flopsy" she called "Flopsy, bring a needle
and help sew up Gordon's pants". "Poor Dads!" said

Jennie "aren't you shockingly bullied? Cross my heart, spit on my finger" she added "I'll never treat my man like this virago" and she pressed Nan's elbow tenderly. Peter smiled uneasily and uncrossed his legs. But Mr. Cockshott was purring as a buzz of feminine interest surrounded him. "I'll tell you a secret, Barrett" he said "Women are like touchy Collie dogs, they need humouring". Peter was about to reply in what he felt to be a suitable man to man vein, when he was startled by finding a large bodkin thrust into his left hand. "Hold that" said Flopsy "and don't sit gaping." The kindness that lay behind her gruff voice was almost unbearable. "You'll have to learn to be useful if you want to earn your bread and butter in this house. No drones here". "Oh for crying out loud" said Nan "Flopsy you're scaring the poor boy into fits". "Peter's not frightened, are you darling?" said Jennie "Why it didn't take him any time to see how much Flopsy's bark meant". Peter laughed and tried to smile at Flopsy. "I shan't eat you up, young man" she said. But Mr. Cockshott was growing restive, his face took on an expression of caricatured thoughtfulness and he bit on his pipe. "Of course, I might appear with no trousers at all" he said "Aesthetically I should be perfectly justified, for I still have a very fine leg. Hygienically—well the weather is very warm and trousers are an undesirable encumbrance. Socially I make my own laws. I have only one hesitation and that is in the moral sphere. I have no doubt at all that the sight of my splendid limbs would cause Mrs. Brasher to become discontented with her own spouse's spindly shanks; and whilst I have the greatest contempt for that horsetoothed, henpecked gentleman, I have also the highest respect for the institution of marriage. No, I must remain a martyr to the cause of public morality". A chorus of laughter greeted this

sally and Nan declared he was impossible, whilst Jennie
dared him to carry out his threats. "Oh, do, Dads, do"
she cried "I'd so adore to see Mrs. Brasher's face. Go on,
I dare you", but Dads just shook his head. "Flopsy shall
make me a kilt in the long winter evenings" he declared.
I'll make you a bag to put your head in if you don't stand
still while I'm patching you" said Flopsy, laughing.
"Heathenish woman, how right they were to give you
that outlandish name". "It's not an outlandish name"
said Jennie "Flopsy's a lovely name. It comes from the
Flopsy Bunnies in *Peter Rabbit*". "It does not" said
Hamish, entering the room. "It is taken from the
immortal English Surrealist Edward Lear and his Mop-
sikon-Flopsikon bear". After what seemed to Peter an
age the family were ready to depart, he would not have
dared to confess to Jennie his relief as he heard the car
disappear down the drive.

Despite all Nan's apologies that the evening meal was
just a picnic, Peter decided that they lived very well; with
the combined produce of the garden, neighbouring farms
and American relations it was clear that austerity had not
seriously touched them. Sweet corn and tunny fish was
followed by roast chicken, and the meal ended with open
apple tart and lemon meringue pie. Everybody ate very
heartily, whilst deploring the hard times in which they
lived. To Mr. Cockshott no régime could be called
civilized that compelled a discriminating palate to take
beer rather than wine with dinner. Hamish was unable to
see what else could result from a sentimental system designed to level down. Flopsy suspected that to get decent
food it would soon be necessary to descend the mines,
where she had no doubt that caviare and foie gras were
being consumed hourly. Nan adored the farmhouse
simplicity of it all and had always wanted to live on such

wholesome fare, but she deplored the disappearance of the old English hospitality which scarcity compelled. Jennie with one eye on Peter remained silent, but in face of such unaccustomed plenty Peter was in no critical mood. Indeed as he sat in an armchair with a cup of Nan's excellent American coffee and a glass of cointreau unearthed by Mr. Cockshott from his treasure house, he did not even feel alarmed that he had been left alone with Hamish.

For a time there was silence as Hamish looked at the evening paper gloomily, then quite suddenly he said "Well we've reached the final point of fantasy. Vitiate the minds or what pass for the minds of the people with education, teach them to read and write, feed their imaginations with sexual and criminal fantasies known as films, and then starve them in order to pay for these delightful erotic celluloids. Circenses without panem it seems". "Yes" said Peter "it's pretty bad. I don't suppose anyone would be the worse for the disappearance of a lot of the films we get from America. But you tend to forget perhaps the routine nature of so many jobs to-day, people need recreation and some emotional outlet". "I don't accept industrialization as an excuse for anything" said Hamish. "We made the machines, we can get rid of them. People seem to forget that our wills are still free. As to recreation, that died out with village life. I don't know quite what you mean by emotional outlet, judging by most films I take it you refer to sexual intercourse, there I'm oldfashioned enough to believe that marriage for the purposes of procreation is still quite an intelligent answer. But if you mean the need for something not purely material, some exercise of the sense of awe, you people killed that when you killed churchgoing". Peter laughed and denied that he was responsible for the decline in Church congregations. "*Do* you go to church?" said Hamish. "No" said Peter "I suppose I incline to agnosticism in religion". "You incline to agnosticism" said Hamish scornfully "which means I suppose that you prefer to believe the latest miracle performed by some B.Sc.London to the authority of 2,000 years". "I don't think the divergence of science and religion is quite the issue nowadays" said Peter as calmly as he could manage "After all so many modern physicists are by no means hostile to religious belief". "Very kind of them I'm sure" said Hamish "In any case I was not talking about what the B.B.C. calls 'belief in God', that is not a thing for discussion really. I was talking of churchgoing. The greatest dereliction of duty in an irresponsible age is the failure of the educated and propertied classes to set an example by attending their parish churches". "You would hardly advocate attendance at church by non-believers". "My dear fellow" said Hamish "all this talk about belief or non-belief is rather crude. A Roman gentleman might privately be a Stoic or an Epicurean but that didn't prevent him from performing his duty to his country by sacrificing to the Gods. We have privileges and we must act accordingly by setting an example to our inferiors". "I think" said Peter angrily "that that view is crazy as well as unchristian". "Yes" said Hamish "so does the *Sunday Express*. I think that the only dignified approach to the modern world *is* to be classed as crazy". Further acrimony was prevented by the appearance of Mr. Cockshott with some papers and Hamish retired.

"Where has Jennie gone?" asked Peter rather restively. "In these unhallowed times" said Mr. Cockshott "even the fairest of women have to partake in the household duties, in short the women of the house are assisting

cook with the washing up". "But can't I help?" asked
Peter. "Good Heavens, my dear boy. No. Let us retain
some of the privileges of our sex. Jennie tells me you
have a taste for literature, so I've brought you a few
occasional writings of mine for a little light bedside
reading". Peter took the offprints with a sincere interest.
"I should very much like to read them" he said. "Thank
you" said Mr. Cockshott "thank you. I project a longer
work—a history of North Cambridgeshire which will be
at once, I hope, a scholarly account of the changing
institutions and a work of literary value and entertain-
ment describing the social scene with its quaint everyday
characters and customs. Unfortunately my position as a
J.P. and a local landlord, though only of course on a
small scale, leaves me less time for writing than I should
like. In any case I am not one who is content with information without style. That's why I'm afraid I quarrel
with our good neighbours the Cambridge Fellows. I find
most of their painstaking researches quite unreadable,
but then I'm neither a pedagogue nor a pedant. On the
other hand, though I believe that imagination must infuse
the pages of history if they are to live, I could not write
what is known as the popular historical biography. I
have too much sense of accuracy and too little interest in
the seamy side of the past to do that, nor have I the requisite standard of vulgarity in my writing. In fact I'm
rather a fish out of water, a fact that is always brought
home to me when I attend the meetings of historical or
antiquarian societies". It seemed to Peter that Mr. Cockshott talked for hours about the various quarrels he had
engaged in with eminent historians and authors, he began
to feel more and more drowsy and the desire to be with
Jennie, to touch and feel her became stronger and
stronger. At last the door was opened and Nan appeared.

"Oh! Gordon" she said "look at poor Peter he's so tired and white. You want to go to bed, don't you?" "I am rather tired after the journey" said Peter, but he hastened to add "It's all been awfully interesting and I'm very much looking forward to reading these articles".

As he walked along the corridor to his room he passed an open door of another bedroom. Inside two figures were locked in each other's arms. He went quickly and, he hoped, silently past. He told himself that he had always known how tremendously fond Jennie was of her brother, but all the same the droop of her body and the force of Hamish's embrace troubled him much that night.

Peter sat in a deck chair after breakfast the next morning attempting to read Mr. Cockshott's account of the Black Death in Little Fromling, but he could not attend to the essay. He felt tired and irritable, for he had slept very poorly. He found himself wondering where Jennie had gone, she had slipped away after breakfast to make the beds, promising to join him in a few minutes, and now nearly an hour had passed. He decided to go and look for her. He found Mr. Cockshott in the morning room writing letters. "Do you know where Jennie is?" he asked. "Ah where indeed?" said Mr. Cockshott "That's what I'm always asking when she's here at the weekends. I never seem to see anything of her. We're all a bit jealous over Jennie. But her independence is part of her charm. She will be free, she won't be monopolized". "I had no intention of monopolizing her. I just wanted to talk to her that's all". "My dear boy I quite understand your feelings and it's very naughty of her to have left her guest like this. But we're rather a crazy family, lacking in the conventions, or rather perhaps I should say we make our own". Peter decided to seek her elsewhere. He went upstairs to his bedroom, there he found Flopsy making

the bed. "You can't come up to your room now" said
Flopsy "The chambermaid's at work". "I was looking
for Jennie". "Well you mustn't look like an angry dog,
you'll never hold Jennie that way. You like her a lot,
don't you?" "I'm very fond of Jennie" said Peter "very
fond indeed". "Good Heavens! I should hope so and
more. Any man in his senses would be head over heels
about Jennie. But there" she added "I'm partial". But
she obviously did not think so. "If it's any satisfaction to
you" said Peter savagely "I'm in love with Jennie and
that's why I want to see her". "Good for you" said
Flopsy. "But don't bite my head off. We Cockshotts are
a crazy crowd, you know, you can't drive us. Well, now
be off. I must make this bed". Peter wandered out into
the garden where he found Nan in an old waterproof
and a battered felt hat making a bonfire. "Have you seen
Jennie?" he asked. "Oh Peter" she said "Has she left you
on your own? No! that's too bad. But there you are
that's the Cockshotts all over, they're completely crazy".
"Don't you find it rather a strain?" asked Peter. "Maybe
at first I did a little, but they're so natural and simple I
love that way of living" for a moment she looked away
from him. "They do ask rather a lot from people" she
said, and her voice sounded for the first time sincere. A
moment later her blue eyes were looking at him with that
frank, open stare which he was beginning to mistrust.
"It's not that really, it's just that they ask a lot of life.
You see they're big people and big people are often kind
of strange to understand". She laid her hand on Peter's
arm "Go see if she's in the Tree House" she said. "It's a
kind of funny old place she and Hamish made when they
were kids and they still love it. It's down at the end of the
garden by the little wood".

Jennie and Hamish were sitting on a wooden platform

up in an elm tree when Peter found them. They were practising tying knots in a piece of rope. Peter's anger must have shown itself for Jennie called out "Welcome, darling, welcome to the Tree House. You ought to make three salaams before you're allowed in, but we'll let you off this time, won't we Hamish?" "Certainly" said Hamish, who also appeared anxious to placate Peter. "I thought you went to Church on Sunday mornings" said Peter. "Everything must give way to the hospitality due to friends" said Hamish with a charming smile. "There was no need to have stayed away for me". "Now, Peter," said Jennie "that's rude after Hamish has been so nice". "We ought to saw some logs" said Hamish "Would you like to give a hand?" "Oh yes do let's" said Jennie "You and Peter can take the double saw, and I'll do the small branches".

Peter did not find it very easy to keep up to Hamish's pace, he got very hot and out of breath, the sawdust kept flying in his face and the teeth of the saw stuck suddenly in the knots of wood so that they were both violently jolted. "I say" said Hamish "I don't think you're very good at this. Perhaps we'd better stop". "No" said Jennie who was angry at Peter's inefficiency "Certainly not, it does Peter good to do things he's not good at". Peter immediately let go off his end of the saw so that it swung sharply round almost cutting off Hamish's arm. "Bloody Hell" said Hamish, but Peter took no notice, he strode rapidly away down the path through the little copse. Jennie ran after him. "Good Heavens, Peter" she called "Whatever is the matter? Don't be such an idiot. Just because I said it was good for you to go on sawing and so it would have been". "It's a great deal more than that" said Peter tensely "as you'd see if you weren't blind with love of your family". "Darling, what has upset you? Surely you aren't annoyed with Hamish, why he's only a child". "I'm well aware of that" said Peter "a vain, spoilt child to be petted and fussed one minute and bullied and ordered about the next. And your father's just as bad. Well I don't want a lot of women petting and bullying me, not Nan, nor your beloved Flopsy, no nor even you". "Peter you're crazy". "Good God! I'm only trying to live up to your family. I've had it ever since I arrived 'The Crazy Cockshotts' and bloody proud of it. I've had it from you and your father, from Flopsy and from Nan, wretched woman she ought to know all about it, and I've had it from your Fascist brother. You're all a damned sight too crazy for me to live up to". Jennie was getting quite out of breath, trying to keep up with Peter's increasing pace. Suddenly she flung herself down in the thick bracken at the side of the path. "Stop! Peter, stop!" she called. Peter stood still over her and she stretched out her hand to him, pulling him down on top of her. Her mouth pressed tightly to his, and her hands stroked his hair, his arms, his back, soothing and caressing him. Gradually his anger died from him and the tension relaxed as in his turn he held her to him.

A Visit in Bad Taste

"HE looks very much older" said Margaret. "It's aged him dreadfully and made him servile."

"I should imagine that prison does tend to kill one's independence" said her husband drily.

"Oh yes that's all very well, Malcolm, you can afford to be rational, to explain away, to account for. But he's my brother and no amount of reasons can make it any better to have him sitting there fingering his tie when he talks, loosening his collar with his finger, deferring every opinion to you, calling old Colonel Gordon sir, jumping up with every move I make. It's like a rather pathetic minor public schoolboy of nineteen applying for a job, and he's sixty, Malcolm, remember that—sixty".

"I think, you know" said Malcolm Tarrant, as he re-placed his glass of port on the little table by his side "that public school has always meant a lot more to Arthur than we can quite understand. The only time that I visited him in Tamcaster I was struck by the importance that they all attached to it. As a bank manager there and a worthy citizen of the town it was in some kind of way a passport to power, not just the place you'd been at school at. And now, I imagine, it's assumed an importance out of all perspective, a kind of lifebuoy to a drowning sailor. We're inclined to imagine prison as peopled with public schoolboys, each with a toothbrush moustache and an assumed military rank, 'ex-public schoolboy gaoled', but they only make so much of it because it's so unusual. God knows what sort of awful snobbery the presence of a 'public schoolman' arouses among the old lags, or the warders too for that matter—people speak so often of the horrors of War but they never mention the most awful of them—the mind of the non-commissioned officer. Depend upon it, whatever snobbery there was, Arthur got full benefit from it".

Margaret's deep, black eyes showed no sign of her distress, only her long upper lip stiffened and the tapir's nose that would have done credit to an Edward Lear drawing showed more white. The firelight shone upon her rich silver brocade evening dress as she rustled and shimmered across the room to place a log on the great open fire. She put the tiny liqueur glass of light emerald —how Malcolm always laughed at her feminine taste for crême de menthe!—upon the mantelpiece between the Chelsea group of Silenus and a country girl and the plain grey bowl filled with coppery and red-gold chrysanthemums.

"If you mean that Arthur is vulgar" she cried "always has been, yes, yes. At least, not always" and her thin lips, so faintly rouged, relaxed into tenderness "not when we were children. But increasingly so. My dear, how could I think otherwise, married to that terrible little woman.— 'How do you keep the servants from thieving, Margaret?' —'Give that class an inch and they'll take an ell'—dreadful, vulgar little Fascist-minded creature".

"Dear Margaret" said Malcolm, and he smiled the special smile of admiring condescension that he kept for his wife's political opinions. "Remember that in Myra's eyes you were a terrible red."

"It isn't a question of politics, Malcolm" said his wife and she frowned—to her husband she was once again the serious minded, simple student he had found so irresistible at Cambridge nearly forty years ago. "It's a question of taste. No, it was a terrible marriage and a terrible life.

It was the one excuse I could make for him at the time. To have lived for so many years against such a background was excuse enough for any crime, yes, even that one. I felt it all through the trial as I sat and watched Myra being the injured wife, with that ghastly family round her".

"That's where we differ" said Malcolm and for a moment his handsome, high cheekboned face with its Roman nose showed all his Covenanting ancestry "I could never excuse his actions. I tried to rid myself of prejudice against them, to see him as a sick man rather than as a criminal" it was not for nothing one felt that the progressive weeklies were so neatly piled on the table beside him "but when he refused psychiatric treatment the whole thing became impossible."

Margaret smiled at her husband maternally as she speared a crystallized orange from its wooden box with the little two pronged fork. "It must be wonderful to have everything all cut and dried like you, darling" she said "only people don't fit into pigeon holes according to the demands of reason. Arthur would never go to a psychoanalyst, you old goose; in the first place he thinks it isn't respectable, and then deep down, of course, he would be frightened of it, he would think it was witchcraft."

"No doubt you're right. No doubt Arthur does still live in the Middle Ages" he moved his cigar dexterously so that the long grey ash fell into the ashtray rather than on to his suit, he narrowed his eyes "I still find his actions disgusting, inexcusable."

"Offences against children" said Margaret and she spoke the phrase in inverted commas, contemptuously "I suppose there is no woman whose blood does not get heated when she reads that in the newspaper. But somehow it all seemed so different when I saw it at the trial. Arthur seemed so shrunken and small, so curiously remote for the principal actor, as though he'd done it all inadvertently.   He probably had, too," she added fiercely, striking the arm of her chair with her hand "in order to forget that dreadful, bright woman—that awful, chromium-plated, cocktail-cabinet, old-oak-lounge home. And then those ghastly people—the parents—there are some kinds of working class people I just cannot take— servile and defiant, obstinate and shifty. I believe every word Arthur said when he told of their menaces, their sudden visits, their demands for money. Oh! they'd had their pound of flesh alright" she said bitterly "in unhappiness and fear.   Even the children, Malcolm, it sounds so moving in the abstract, poor little creatures not comprehending, their whole lives distorted by a single incident. When Rupert and Jane were little, I used to think that if anyone harmed them I would put his eyes out with hot irons. But these children weren't like that— that cretinous boy with the sudden look of cunning in his eyes and that awful, painted, oversexed girl."

"It's a pity you ever went to the trial" said Malcolm, but Margaret could not agree. "I had to suffer it all" she cried "it was the only way. But that Dostoevskeyan mood is over. I don't want any more of it, I want it to be finished". She fitted a cigarette into one of the little cardboard holders that stood in a glass jar on her work-table, then suddenly she turned on her husband fiercely "Why has he come here? Why? Why?" she cried.

"I imagine because he's lonely" said Malcolm.

"Of course he is. What can be expected? But he'll be just as lonely here. We aren't his sort of people, Malcolm. Oh! Not just because of what's happened, we never have been. This isn't his kind of house". She thought with

pleasure of all they had built up there—the taste, the
tolerance, the ease of living, the lack of dogmatism. Her
eyes lighted on the Chelsea and the Meissen figures, the
John drawings, the Spanish metalwork, the little pale
yellow spinet—eclectic but good. Her ears heard once
more Ralph Tarrant telling them of his ideas for Hamlet,
Mrs. Doyle speaking of her life with the great man,
Professor Crewe describing his theory of obsolete ideas,
Dr. Modjka his terrible meeting with Hitler. Arthur had
no place there.

"You want me to ask him to go" said Malcolm slowly.
Margaret bent over the fire, crouching on a stool in the
hearth, holding out her hands to the warmth. "Yes" she
said in a low voice "I do." "Before he's found his feet?"
Malcolm was puzzled. "He knows I think that he must
move eventually, but for the moment. . . ." "The
moment!" broke in Margaret savagely. "If he stays
now he stays for ever, I'm as certain of that as that I
stand. Don't ask me *how* I know, but I do." "Ah! well.
It won't be a very pleasant talk" said her husband "but
perhaps it will be for the best."

Only the frou-frou of Margaret's skirt broke the silence as she moved about the room, rearranging the
sprigs of winter jasmine, drawing the heavy striped satin
curtains across to cover a crack of light. Suddenly she sat
down again on the stool and began to unwrap some sewing from a little silk bundle.

"I think the last chapter of Walter's book very pretentious" she said in a voice harder and clearer than
normal. "He's at his worst when he's doing the great
Panjandrum".

"Poor Walter" said Malcolm "You can't go on playing
Peter Pan *and* speak with the voice of authority. . . ."

They had not long been talking, when Arthur came in.

His suit looked over pressed, his tie was too "club", his hair had too much brilliantine for a man of his age. All his actions were carried out overconsciously, with military precision; as he sat down he jerked up his trousers to preserve the crease, he removed a white handkerchief from his shirtcuff, wiped his little toothbrush moustache and cleared his throat—"Sorry to have been so long" he said "Nature's call, you know". Malcolm smiled wryly and Margaret winced.

"You don't take sugar, do you Arthur?" she said as she handed him his coffee.

"Will you have a glass of port, old man?" asked Malcolm, adapting his phraseology to his brother-in-law.

"Oh! thanks very much" said Arthur in quick, nervous tones, fingering his collar. Then feeling that such diffidence was unsuitable, he added "Port, eh? Very fruity, very tasty".

There was a long pause, then Margaret and Malcolm spoke at once.

"I've just been saying that Walter Howard's new book. . . ." she began.

"Did you have an opportunity to look at the trees we've planted?" said Malcolm. Then, as Margaret, blushing, turned her head away, he continued "We ought really to have more trees down, if this fuel shortage is going to materialize. I'll get on to Bowers about it."

"Oh not this week, darling" said Margaret "Mrs. Bowers is away with her mother who's ill and young Peter's has got flu. Poor Bowers is terribly overworked."

"Next week then" said Malcolm "I must say I've never known such a set for illness".

"Give them an inch and they'll take an ell" said Arthur.

The reiteration of her sister-in-law's phrase enraged Margaret. "What nonsense you do talk, Arthur" she cried "I should have thought the last few months would have taught you some sense". She blushed scarlet as she realized what she had said, then more gently she added "You don't know the Bowers. Why Mrs. Bowers is the best friend I have round here".

Arthur felt the old order was on its mettle, he was not prepared to be placated. "I'm afraid my respect for your precious British workmen has not been increased where I come from" he said defiantly.

"I doubt if you saw the British workman at his best in prison" said Malcolm carefully, and as his brother-in-law was about to continue the argument, he added "No, Arthur, let's leave it at that—Margaret and I have our own ideas on these things and we're too old to change them now."

Arthur's defiance vanished. He fingered the knot of his tie and mumbled something about "respecting them for it". There was a silence for some minutes, then Malcolm said abruptly "Where do you plan to go from here?" Arthur was understood to say that he hadn't thought about it.

"I think you should" said Malcolm "Why don't you go abroad?"

"The Colonies?" questioned Arthur with a little laugh.

"I know it's conventional, but why not? You can always count on me if you need any money."

Arthur did not speak for a moment. Then "You *want* me to go from here?" he asked. Margaret was determined to fight her own battle, so "Yes, Arthur" she replied "You must. It won't do here, we don't fit in together."

"I doubt if *I* fit in anywhere" Arthur's voice was bitter.

Malcolm would have dispelled the mood with a "nonsense, old man", but Margaret again took up the task. "No, Malcolm, perhaps he's right" suddenly her voice became far away, with a dramatic note. "When Malcolm was at the Ministry in London during the raids and Rupert was flying over Germany, I had to realize that they might both be killed and, then, of course *I* wouldn't have fitted in. I took my precautions. I always carried something that would finish me off quickly if I needed it. Remember, Arthur, if anything should happen I shall always understand and respect you."

Malcolm looked away, embarrassed. These moments of self-dramatization of Margaret's made him feel that he had married beneath him.

Arthur sat, thinking—the colonies or suicide, neither seemed to be what he was needing.

"Well" he said finally "I'm very tired, I'll be toddling off to bed, I think. A real long night'll do me good."

Margaret got up and stroked his hair.

"Ee," he said "it's a moocky do, lass, as Nurse used to say".

This direct appeal to sentiment repelled her "You'll find whisky and a syphon in your room" she said formally.

"Yes, have a good nightcap" said Malcolm to the erect over military back of his brother-in-law.

"Thank God that's over" he sighed a few minutes later. "Poor old Arthur. I expect he'll find happiness sometime, somewhere."

"No, Malcolm" said Margaret fiercely "it's been an unpleasant business, but if it's not to turn sour on us, we've got to face it. Arthur will *never* be happy, he's rotten, dead. But we aren't, and if we're going to live, we can't afford to let his rottenness infect us."

Malcolm stared at his wife with admiration—to face reality, that was obviously the way to meet these things, not to try to escape. He thought for a few minutes of what she had said—of Arthur's rottenness—socially and personally—and of all that they stood for—individually alive, socially progressive. But for all the realism of her view, it somehow did not satisfy him. He remained vaguely uneasy the whole evening.

Raspberry Jam

"**H**OW are your funny friends at Potter's Farm, Johnnie?" asked his aunt from London.

"Very well, thank you, Aunt Eva" said the little boy in the window in a high prim voice. He had been drawing faces on his bare knee and now put down the indelible pencil. The moment that he had been dreading all day had arrived. Now they would probe and probe with their silly questions and the whole story of that dreadful tea party with his old friends would come tumbling out. There would be scenes and abuse and the old ladies would be made to suffer further. This he could not bear, for although he never wanted to see them again and had come, in brooding over the afternoon's events, almost to hate them, to bring them further misery, to be the means of their disgrace would be worse than any of the horrible things that had already happened. Apart from his fear of what might follow he did not intend to pursue the conversation himself, for he disliked his aunt's bright patronizing tone. He knew that she felt ill at ease with children and would soon lapse into that embarrassing "leg pulling" manner which some grown ups used. For himself, he did not mind this but if she made silly jokes about the old ladies at Potter's Farm he would get angry and then Mummy would say all that about his having to learn to take a joke and about his being highly strung and where could he have got it from, not from her.

But he need not have feared. For though the grown-ups continued to speak of the old ladies as "Johnnie's friends", the topic soon became a general one. Many of the things the others said made the little boy bite his lip, but he was able to go on drawing on his knee with the feigned abstraction of a child among adults.

"My dear", said Johnnie's mother to her sister "you really must meet them. They're the *most* wonderful pair of freaks. They live in a great barn of a farmhouse. The inside's like a museum, full of old junk mixed up with some really lovely things all mouldering to pieces. The family's been there for hundreds of years and they're madly proud of it. They won't let anyone do a single thing for them, although they're both well over sixty, and of course the result is that the place is in the most *frightful* mess. It's really rather ghastly and one oughtn't to laugh, but if you could *see* them, my dear. The elder one, Marian, wears a long tweed skirt almost to the ankles, she had a terrible hunting accident or something, and a school blazer. The younger one's said to have been a beauty, but she's really rather sinister now, inches thick in enamel and rouge and dressed in all colours of the rainbow, with dyed red hair which is constantly falling down. Of course, Johnnie's made tremendous friends with them and I must say they've been immensely kind to him, but what Harry will say when he comes back from Germany, I can't think. As it *is*, he's always complaining that the child is too much with women and has no friends of his own age."

"I don't honestly think you need worry about that, Grace" said her brother Jim, assuming the attitude of the sole male in the company, for of the masculinity of old Mr. Codrington their guest he instinctively made little. "Harry ought to be very pleased with the way old Miss Marian's encouraged Johnnie's cricket and riding; it's pretty uphill work, too. Johnnie's not exactly a Don Bradman or a Gordon Richards, are you, old man? I like the old girl, personally. She's got a bee in her bonnet about the Bolsheviks, but she's stood up to those damned council people about the drainage like a good 'un; she does no end for the village people as well and says very little about it."

"I don't like the sound of 'doing good to the village' very much" said Eva "it usually means patronage and disappointed old maids meddling in other people's affairs. It's only in villages like this that people can go on serving out sermons with gifts of soup".

"Curiously enough, Eva old dear", Jim said, for he believed in being rude to his progressive sister, "in this particular case you happen to be wrong. Miss Swindale is extremely broadminded. You remember, Grace," he said, addressing his other sister "what she said about giving money to old Cooper, when the rector protested it would only go on drink—'You have a perfect right to consign us all to hell, rector, but you must allow us the choice of how we get there'. Serve him damn well right for interfering too."

"Well, Jim darling" said Grace "I must say she could hardly have the nerve to object to drink—the poor old thing has the most dreadful bouts herself. Sometimes when I can't get gin from the grocer's it makes me absolutely livid to think of all that secret drinking and they say it only makes her more and more gloomy. All the same I suppose *I* should drink if I had a sister like Dolly. It must be horrifying when one's family proud like she is to have such a skeleton in the cupboard. I'm sure there's going to be the most awful trouble in the village about Dolly before she's finished. You've heard the squalid story about young Tony Calkett, haven't you? My dear, he went round there to fix the lights and apparently Dolly invited him up to her bedroom to have a cherry brandy of all things and made the *most* unfortunate proposals. Of course I know she's been very lonely and it's all a ghastly tragedy really, but Mrs. Calkett's a terribly silly little woman and a very jealous mother and she won't see it that way at all. The awful thing is that both the Miss Swindales give me the creeps rather. I have a dreadful feeling when I'm with them that I don't know who's the keeper and who's the lunatic. In fact, Eva my dear, they're both really rather horrors and I suppose I ought never to let Johnnie go near them."

"I think you have no cause for alarm, Mrs. Allingham" put in old Mr. Codrington in a purring voice. He had been waiting for some time to take the floor, and now that he had got it he did not intend to relinquish it. Had it not been for the small range of village society he would not have been a visitor at Mrs. Allingham's, for, as he frequently remarked, if there was one thing he deplored more than her vulgarity it was her loquacity. "No one delights in scandal more than I do, but it is always a little distorted, a trifle *exageré*, indeed where would be its charm, if it were not so! No doubt Miss Marian has her solaces, but she remains a noble-hearted woman. No doubt Miss Dolly is often a trifle naughty" he dwelt on this word caressingly "but she really only uses the privilege of one, who has been that rare thing, a beautiful woman. As for Tony Calkett it is really time that that young man ceased to be so unnecessarily virginal. If my calculations are correct, and I have every reason to think they are, he must be twenty-two, an age at which modesty should have been put behind one long since. No, dear Mrs. Allingham, you should rejoice that Johnnie has been given the friendship of two women who can still, in this vulgar age, be honoured with a name that, for all that it has been cheapened and degraded, one is still proud to bestow—the name of a lady". Mr. Codrington threw his head back and stared round the room as though defying anyone to deny him his own right to this name. "Miss Marian will encourage him in the manlier virtues, Miss Dolly in the arts. Her own water colours, though perhaps lacking in strength, are not to be despised. She has a fine sense of colour, though I could wish that she was a little less bold with it in her costume. Nevertheless with that red gold hair there is something splendid about her appearance, something especially wistful to an old man like myself. Those peacock blue linen gowns take me back through Conder's fans and Whistler's rooms to Rossetti's Mona Vanna. Unfortunately as she gets older the linen is not overclean. We are given a Mona Vanna with the collected dust of age, but surely", he added with a little cackle "it is dirt that lends patina to a picture. It is interesting that you should say you are uncertain which of the two sisters is a trifle peculiar, because, in point of fact, both have been away, as they used to phrase it in the servants' hall of my youth. Strange" he mused "that one's knowledge of the servants' hall should always belong to the period of one's infancy, be, as it were, eternally outmoded. I have no conception of how they may speak of an asylum in the servants' hall of to-day. No doubt Johnnie could tell us. But, of course, I forget that social progress has removed the servants' hall from the ken of all but the most privileged children. I wonder now whether that is a loss or a blessing in disguise".

"A blessing without any doubt at all" said Aunt Eva, irrepressible in the cause of Advance. "Think of all the appalling inhibitions we acquired from servants' chatter. I had an old nurse who was always talking about ghosts and dead bodies and curses on the family in a way that must have set up terrible phobias in me. I still have those ugly, morbid nightmares about spiders" she said, turning to Grace.

"I refuse" said Mr. Codrington in a voice of great contempt, for he was greatly displeased at the interruption, "to believe that any dream of yours could be ugly; morbid, perhaps, but with a sense of drama and artistry that would befit the dreamer. I confess that if I have inhibitions, and I trust I have many, I cling to them. I should not wish to give way unreservedly to what is so unattractively called the libido, it suggests a state of affairs in which beach pyjamas are worn and jitterbugging is compulsory. No, let us retain the fantasies, the imaginative games of childhood, even at the expense of a little fear, for they are the true magnificence of the springtime of life".

"Darling Mr. Codrington" cried Grace "I do pray and hope you're right. It's exactly what I keep on telling myself about Johnnie, but I really don't know. Johnnie, darling, run upstairs and fetch mummy's bag". But his mother need not have been so solicitous about Johnnie's overhearing what she had to say, for the child had already left the room. "There you are, Eva", she said "he's the strangest child. He slips away without so much as a word I must say he's very good at amusing himself, but I very much wonder if all the funny games he plays aren't very bad for him. He's certainly been very peculiar lately, strange silences and sudden tears, and, my dear, the awful nightmares he has! About a fortnight ago, after he'd been at tea with the Miss Swindales, I don't know whether it was something he'd eaten there, but he made the most awful sobbing noise in the night. Sometimes I think it's just temper, like Harry. The other day at tea I only offered him some jam, my best home-made raspberry too, and he just screamed at me".

K

"You should take him to a child psychologist" said her sister.

"Well, darling, I expect you're right. It's so difficult to know whether they're frauds, everyone recommends somebody different. I'm sure Harry would disapprove too, and then think of the expense. . . . You know how desperately poor we are, although I think I manage as well as anyone could". . . . At this point Mr. Codrington took a deep breath and sat back, for on the merits of her household management Grace Allingham was at her most boring and could by no possible stratagem be restrained.

Upstairs, in the room which had been known as the nursery until his eleventh birthday, but was now called his bedroom, Johnnie was playing with his farm animals. The ritual involved in the game was very complicated and had a long history. It was on his ninth birthday that he had been given the farm set by his father. "Something a bit less babyish than those woolly animals of yours" he had said, and Johnnie had accepted them, since they made in fact no difference whatever to the games he played; games at which could Major Allingham have guessed he would have been distinctly puzzled. The little ducks, pigs and cows of lead no more remained themselves in Johnnie's games than had the pink woollen sheep and green cloth horses of his early childhood. Johnnie's world was a strange compound of the adult world in which he had always lived and a book world composed from Grimm, the Arabian Nights, Alice's adventures, natural history books and more recently the novels of Dickens and Jane Austen. His imagination was taken by anything odd—strange faces, strange names, strange animals, strange voices and catchphrases—all these appeared in his games. The black pig and the white duck were keeping a hotel; the black pig was called that funny name of Granny's friend—Mrs. Gudgeon-Rogers. She was always holding her skirt tight round the knees and warming her bottom over the fire—like Mrs. Coates, and whenever anyone in the hotel asked for anything she would reply "Darling, I can't stop now. I've simply got to fly," like Aunt Sophie, and then she would fly out of the window. The duck was an Echidna, or Spiny Ant-eater who wore a picture hat and a fish train like in the picture of Aunt Eleanor; she used to weep a lot, because, like Granny, when she described her games of bridge, she was "vulnerable" and she would yawn at the hotel guests and say "Lord I am tired" like Lydia Bennet. The two collie dogs had "been asked to leave", like in the story of Mummy's friend Gertie who "got tight" at the Hunt Ball, they were going to be divorced and were consequently wearing "co-respondent shoes". The lady collie who was called Minnie Mongelheim kept on saying "That chaps' got a proud stomach. Let him eat chaff" like Mr. F's Aunt in Little Dorrit. The sheep, who always played the part of a bore, kept on and on talking like Daddy about "leg cuts and fine shots to cover"; sometimes when the rest of the animal guests got too bored the sheep would change into Grandfather Graham and tell a funny story about a Scotsman so that they were bored in a different way. Finally the cat who was a grand vizier and worked by magic would say "All the ways round here belong to me" like the Red Queen and he would have all the guests torn in pieces and flayed alive until Johnnie felt so sorry for them that the game would come to an end. Mummy was already saying that he was getting too old for the farm animals: one always seemed to be getting too old for something. In fact the animals were

no longer necessary to Johnnie's games, for most of the
time now he liked to read and when he wanted to play
games he could do so in his head without the aid of any
toys, but he hated the idea of throwing things away
because they were no longer needed. Mummy and Daddy
were always throwing things away and never thinking of
their feelings. When he had been much younger Mummy
had given him an old petticoat to put in the dustbin, but
Johnnie had taken it to his room and hugged it and cried
over it, because it was no longer wanted. Daddy had
been very upset. Daddy was always being upset at what
Johnnie did. Only the last time that he was home there
had been an awful row, because Johnnie had tried to
make up like old Mrs. Langdon and could not wash the
blue paint off his eyes. Daddy had beaten him and looked
very hurt all day and said to Mummy that he'd "rather see
him dead than grow up a cissie". No it was better not to
do imitations oneself, but to leave it to the animals.

This afternoon, however, Johnnie was not attending
seriously to his game, he was sitting and thinking of what
the grown ups had been saying and of how he would
never see his friends, the old ladies, again, and of how he
never, never wanted to. This irrevocable separation lay like
a black cloud over his mind, a constant darkness which
was lit up momentarily by forks of hysterical horror, as
he remembered the nature of their last meeting.

The loss of this friendship was a very serious one to the
little boy. It had met so completely the needs and loneliness which are always great in a child isolated from other
children and surrounded by unimaginative adults. In a
totally unself-conscious way, half-crazy as they were and
half crazy even though the child sensed them to be, the
Misses Swindale possessed just those qualities of which
Johnnie felt most in need. To begin with they were odd

and fantastic and highly coloured, and more important still they believed that such peculiarities were nothing to be ashamed of, indeed were often a matter for pride. "How delightfully odd", Miss Dolly would say in her drawling voice, when Johnnie told her how the duck-billed platypus had chosen spangled tights when Queen Alexandra had ordered her to be shot from a cannon at Brighton Pavilion. "What a delightfully extravagant creature that duckbilled platypus is, Caro Gabriele", for Miss Dolly had brought back a touch of Italian here and there from her years in Florence, whilst in Johnnie she fancied a likeness to the angel Gabriel. In describing her own dresses, too, which she would do for hours on end, extravagance was her chief commendation, "as for that gold and silver brocade ball dress" she would say and her voice would sink to an awed whisper "it was richly fantastic". To Miss Marian, with her more brusque, masculine nature, Johnnie's imaginative powers were a matter of far greater wonder than to her sister and she treated them with even greater respect. In her bluff, simple way like some old fashioned religious army officer or overgrown but solemn schoolboy, she too admired the eccentric and unusual. "What a lark!" she would say, when Johnnie told her how the Crown Prince had slipped in some polar bears dressed in pink ballet skirts to sing "Ta Ra Ra boomdeay" in the middle of a boring school concert which his royal duties had forced him to attend. "What a nice chap he must be to know". In talking of her late father, the general, whose memory she wor-shipped and of whom she had a never ending flow of anecdotes, she would give an instance of his warm-hearted but distinctly eccentric behaviour and say in her gruff voice "Wasn't it rum? That's the bit I like best". But in neither of the sisters was there the least trace of

that self conscious whimsicality which Johnnie had met
and hated in so many grown ups. They were the first
people he had met who liked what he liked and as he liked
it.

Their love of lost causes and their defence of the
broken, the worn out and the forgotten met a deep demand in his nature, which had grown almost sickly
sentimental in the dead, practical world of his home.
He loved the disorder of the old eighteenth century
farm house, the collection of miscellaneous objects of all
kinds that littered the rooms, and thoroughly sympathized
with the sisters' magpie propensity to collect dress ends,
feathers, string, old whistles and broken cups. He grew
excited with them in their fights to prevent drunken old
men being taken to workhouses and cancerous old
women to hospitals, though he sensed something crazy
in their constant fear of intruders, bolsheviks and prying
doctors. He would often try to change the conversation
when Miss Marian became excited about spies in the
village, or told him of how torches had been flashing all
night in the garden and of how the vicar was slandering
her father's memory in a whispering campaign. He felt
deeply embarrassed when Miss Dolly insisted on looking
into all the cupboards and behind the curtains to see, as
she said "if there were any eyes or ears where they were
not wanted. For, Caro Gabriele, those who hate beauty
are many and strong, those who love it are few".

It was, above all, their kindness and their deep affection
which held the love starved child. His friendship with
Miss Dolly had been almost instantaneous. She soon
entered into his fantasies with complete intimacy, and he
was spellbound by her stories of the gaiety and beauty of
Mediterranean life. They would play dressing up games
together and enacted all his favourite historical scenes.

She helped him with his French, too, and taught him Italian words with lovely sounds; she praised his painting and helped him to make costume designs for some of his "characters". With Miss Marian, at first, there had been much greater difficulty. She was an intensely shy woman and took refuge behind a rather forbidding bluntness of manner. Her old-fashioned military airs and general "manly" tone, copied from her father, with which she approached small boys, reminded Johnnie too closely of his own father. "Head up, me lad" she would say "shoulders straight". Once he had come very near to hating her, when after an exhibition of his absentmindedness she had said "Take care, Johnnie head in the air. You'll be lost in the clouds, me' lad, if you're not careful". But the moment after she had won his heart for ever, when with a little chuckle she continued "Jolly good thing if you are, you'll learn things up there that we shall never know". On her side, as soon as she saw that she had won his affection, she lost her shyness and proceeded impulsively to load him with kindnesses. She loved to cook his favourite dishes for him and give him his favourite fruit from their kitchen garden. Her admiration for his precocity and imagination was open eyed and childlike. Finally they had found a common love of Dickens and Jane Austen, which she had read with her father, and now they would sit for hours talking over the characters in their favourite books.

Johnnie's affection for them was intensely protective, and increased daily as he heard and saw the contempt and dislike with which they were regarded by many persons in the village. The knowledge that "they had been away" was nothing new to him when Mr. Codrington had revealed it that afternoon. Once Miss Dolly had told him how a foolish doctor had advised her to go into a home "for you know, caro, ever since I returned to these grey skies my health has not been very good. People here think me strange, I cannot attune myself to the cold northern soul. But it was useless to keep me there, I need beauty and warmth of colour, and there it was so drab. The people, too, were unhappy crazy creatures and I missed my music so dreadfully". Miss Marian had spoken more violently of it on one of her "funny" days, when from the depredations caused by the village boys to the orchard she had passed on to the strange man she had found spying in her father's library and the need for a high wall round the house to prevent people peering through the telescopes from Mr. Hatton's house opposite. "They're frightened of us, though, Johnnie," she had said, "I'm too honest for them and Dolly's too clever. They're always trying to separate us. Once they took me away against my will. They couldn't keep me, I wrote to all sorts of big pots, friends of father's, you know, and they had to release me". Johnnie realized, too, that when his mother had said that she never knew which was the keeper, she had spoken more truly than she understood. Each sister was constantly alarmed for the other and anxious to hide the other's defects from an un-understanding world. Once when Miss Dolly had been telling him a long story about a young waiter who had slipped a note into her hand the last time she had been in London, Miss Marian called Johnnie into the kitchen to look at some pies she had made. Later she had told him not to listen if Dolly said "soppy things" because being so beautiful she did not realize that she was no longer young. Another day when Miss Marian had brought in the silver framed photo of her father in full dress uniform and had asked Johnnie to swear an oath to clear the general's memory in the village, Miss Dolly had begun to play a mazurka on the piano. Later, she too, had warned Johnnie not to take too much notice when her sister got excited. "She lives a little too much in the past. Gabriele. She suffered very much when our father died. Poor Marian, it is a pity perhaps that she is so good, she has had too little of the pleasures of life. But we must love her very much, caro, very much".

Johnnie had sworn to himself to stand by them and to fight the wicked people who said they were old and useless and in the way. But now, since that dreadful tea-party, he could not fight for them any longer, for he knew why they had been shut up and felt that it was justified. In a sense, too, he understood that it was to protect others that they had to be restrained, for the most awful memory of all that terrifying afternoon was the thought that he had shared with pleasure for a moment in their wicked game.

It was certainly most unfortunate that Johnnie should have been invited to tea on that Thursday, for the Misses Swindale had been drinking heavily on and off for the preceding week, and were by that time in a state of mental and nervous excitement that rendered them far from normal. A number of events had combined to produce the greatest sense of isolation in these old women whose sanity in any event hung by a precarious thread. Miss Marian had been involved in an unpleasant scene with the vicar over the new hall for the Young People's Club. She was, as usual, providing the cash for the building and felt extremely happy and excited at being consulted about the decorations. Though she did not care for the vicar, she set out to see him, determined that she would accommodate herself to changing times. In any case, since she

was the benefactress, it was, she felt, particularly necessary that she should take a back seat, to have imposed her
wishes in any way would have been most illbred. It was
an unhappy chance that caused the vicar to harp upon the
need for new fabrics for the chairs and even to digress
upon the ugliness of the old upholstery, for these chairs
had come from the late General Swindale's library. Miss
Marian was immediately reminded of her belief that the
vicar was attempting secretly to blacken her father's
memory, nor was the impression corrected when he tact-
lessly suggested that the question of her father's taste was
unimportant and irrelevant. She was more deeply wounded still to find in the next few days that the village shared
the vicar's view that she was attempting to dictate to the
boys' club by means of her money. "After all", as Mrs.
Grove at the Post Office said, "it's not only the large
sums that count, Miss Swindale, it's all the boys' six-
pences that they've saved up". "You've too much of
your father's ways in you, that's the trouble, Miss Swindale," said Mr. Norton, who was famous for his bluntness "and they won't do nowadays".

She had returned from this unfortunate morning's
shopping to find Mrs. Calkett on the doorstep. Now the
visit of Mrs. Calkett was not altogether unexpected, for
Miss Marian had guessed from chance remarks of her
sister's that something "unfortunate" had happened with
young Tony. When, however, the sharp-faced unpleasant little woman began to complain about Miss
Dolly with innuendos and veiledly coarse suggestions,
Miss Marian could stand it no longer and drove her away
harshly. "How dare you speak about my sister in that
disgusting way, you evil minded little woman" she said.
"You'd better be careful or you'll find yourself charged
with libel". When the scene was over, she felt very tired.

It was dreadful of course that anyone so mean and cheap should speak thus of anyone so fine and beautiful as Dolly, but it was also dreadful that Dolly should have made such a scene possible.

Things were not improved, therefore, when Dolly returned from Brighton at once elevated by a new conquest and depressed by its subsequent results. It seemed that the new conductor on the Southdown "that charming dark Italian looking boy I was telling you about, my dear" had returned her a most intimate smile and pressed her hand when giving her change. Her own smiles must have been embarrassingly intimate, for a woman in the next seat had remarked loudly to her friend, "These painted old things. Really, I wonder the men don't smack their faces". "I couldn't help smiling", remarked Miss Dolly "she was so evidently *jaloux*, my dear. I'm glad to say the conductor did not hear, for no doubt he would have felt it necessary to come to my defence, he was so completely *épris*". But, for once, Miss Marian was too vexed to play ball, she turned on her sister and roundly condemned her conduct, ending up by accusing her of bringing misery to them both and shame to their father's memory. Poor Miss Dolly just stared in bewilderment, her baby blue eyes round with fright, tears washing the mascara from her eyelashes in black streams down the wrinkled vermilion of her cheeks. Finally she ran crying up to her room.

That night both the sisters began to drink heavily. Miss Dolly lay like some monstrous broken doll, her red hair streaming over her shoulders, her corsets unloosed and her fat body poking out of an old pink velvet ball dress—pink with red hair was always so audacious—through the most unexpected places in bulges of thick blue-white flesh. She sipped at glass after glass of gin,

sometimes staring into the distance with bewilderment
that she should find herself in such a condition, sometimes leering pruriently at some pictures of Johnny Weis-
muller in swimsuits that she had cut out of *Film Weekly*.
At last she began to weep to think that she had sunk to
this. Miss Marian sat at her desk and drank more deliberately from a cut glass decanter of brandy. She read
solemnly through her father's letters, their old-fashioned,
earnest Victorian sentiments swimming ever more wildly
before her eyes. But, at last, she, too, began to weep as
she thought of how his memory would be quite gone
when she passed away, and of how she had broken the
promise that she had made to him on his deathbed to
stick to her sister through thick and thin.

So they continued for two or three days with wild
spasms of drinking and horrible, sober periods of remorse. They cooked themselves odd scraps in the kitchen, littering the house with unwashed dishes and cups,
but never speaking, always avoiding each other. They
didn't change their clothes or wash, and indeed made
little alteration in their appearance. Miss Dolly put fresh
rouge on her cheeks periodically and some pink roses in
her hair which hung there wilting; she was twice sick
over the pink velvet dress. Miss Marian put on an old
scarlet hunting waistcoat of her father's, partly out of
maudlin sentiment and partly because she was cold. Once
she fell on the stairs and cut her forehead against the
banisters; the red and white handkerchief which she tied
round her head gave her the appearance of a tipsy pirate.
On the fourth day, the sisters were reconciled and sat in
Miss Dolly's room. That night they slept, lying heavily
against each other on Miss Dolly's bed, open-mouthed
and snoring, Miss Marian's deep guttural rattle contrasting with Miss Dolly's highpitched whistle. They

awoke on Thursday morning, much sobered, to the realization that Johnnie was coming to tea that afternoon.

It was characteristic that neither spoke a word of the late debauch. Together they went out into the hot July sunshine to gather raspberries for Johnnie's tea. But the nets in the kitchen garden had been disarranged and the birds had got the fruit. The awful malignity of this chance event took some time to pierce through the fuddled brains of the two ladies, as they stood there grotesque and obscene in their staring pink and clashing red, with their heavy pouchy faces and blood-shot eyes showing up in the hard, clear light of the sun. But when the realization did get home it seemed to come as a confirmation of all the beliefs of persecution which had been growing throughout the drunken orgy. There is little doubt that they were both a good deal mad when they returned to the house.

Johnnie arrived punctually at four o'clock, for he was a small boy of exceptional politeness. Miss Marian opened the door to him, and he was surprised at her appearance in her red bandana and her scarlet waistcoat, and especially by her voice which, though friendly and gruff as usual, sounded thick and flat. Miss Dolly, too, looked more than usually odd with one eye closed in a kind of perpetual wink, and with her pink dress falling off her shoulders. She kept on laughing in a silly, high giggle. The shock of discovering that the raspberries were gone had driven them back to the bottle and they were both fairly drunk. They pressed upon the little boy, who was thirsty after his walk, two small glasses in succession, one of brandy, the other of gin, though in their sober mood the ladies would have died rather than have seen their little friend take strong liquor. The drink soon combined with the heat of the day and the smell of vomit that hung around the room to make Johnnie feel most strange. The walls of the room seemed to be closing in and the floor to be moving up and down like sea waves. The ladies' faces came up at him suddenly and then receded, now Miss Dolly's with great blobs of blue and scarlet and her eyes winking and leering, now Miss Marian's a huge white mass with her moustache grown large and black. He was only conscious by fits and starts of what they were doing or saying. Sometimes he would hear Miss Marian speaking in a flat, slow monotone. She seemed to be reading out her father's letters, snatches of which came to him clearly and then faded away. "There is so much to be done in our short sojourn on this earth, so much that may be done for good, so much for evil. Let us earnestly endeavour to keep the good steadfastly before us", then suddenly "Major Campbell has told me of his decision to leave the regiment. I pray God hourly that he may have acted in full consideration of the Higher Will to which. . . .", and once grotesquely, "Your Aunt Maud was here yesterday, she is a maddening woman and I consider it a just judgment upon the Liberal party that she should espouse its cause". None of these phrases meant anything to the little boy, but he was dimly conscious that Miss Marian was growing excited, for he heard her say "That was our father. As Shakespeare says 'He was a man take him all in all' Johnnie. We loved him, but there were those who sought to destroy him, for he was too big for them. But their day is nearly ended. Always remember that, Johnnie". It was difficult to hear all that the elder sister said, for Miss Dolly kept on drawling and giggling in his ear about a black charmeuse evening gown she had worn, and a young donkeyboy she had danced with in the fiesta at Asti. "*E come era bello, caro Gabriele, come era bello.* And afterwards . . . but

I must spare the ears of one so young the details of the *arte dell' amore*" she added with a giggle and then with drunken dignity "it would not be immodest I think to mention that his skin was like velvet. Only a few lire, too, just imagine". All this, too, was largely meaningless to the boy, though he remembered it in later years.

For a while he must have slept, since he remembered that later he could see and hear more clearly though his head ached terribly. Miss Dolly was seated at the piano playing a little jig and bobbing up and down like a mountainous pink blancmange, whilst Miss Marian more than ever like a pirate was dancing some sort of a hornpipe. Suddenly Miss Dolly stopped playing. "Shall we show him the prisoner?" she said solemnly. "Head up, shoulders straight", said Miss Marian in a parody of her old manner, "you're going to be very honoured, me' lad. Promise you'll never betray that honour. You shall see one of the enemy punished. Our father gave us close instructions 'Do good to all' he said 'but if you catch one of the enemy, remember you are a soldier's daughters.' We shall obey that command." Meanwhile Miss Dolly had returned from the kitchen, carrying a little bird which was pecking and clawing at the net in which it had been caught and shrilling incessantly—it was a little bullfinch. "You're a very beautiful little bird", Miss Dolly whispered, "with lovely soft pink feathers and pretty grey wings. But you're a very naughty little bird too, *tanto cattivo*. You came and took the fruit from us which we'd kept for our darling Gabriele". She began feverishly to pull the rose breast feathers from the bird, which piped more loudly and squirmed. Soon little trickles of red blood ran down among the feathers. "Scarlet and pink a very daring combination", Miss Dolly cried. Johnnie watched from his chair, his heart beating fast. Suddenly Miss Marian stepped forward and holding the bird's head she thrust a pin into its eyes. "We don't like spies round here looking at what we are doing", she said in her flat, gruff voice "When we find them we teach them a lesson so that they don't spy on us again". Then she took out a little pocket knife and cut into the bird's breast; its wings were beating more feebly now and its claws only moved spasmodically, whilst its chirping was very faint. Little yellow and white strings of entrails began to peep out from where she had cut. "Oh!" cried Miss Dolly, "I like the lovely colours, I don't like these worms". But Johnnie could bear it no longer, white and shaking he jumped from his chair and seizing the bird he threw it on the floor and then he stamped on it violently until it was nothing but a sodden crimson mass. "Oh, Gabriele, what have you done? You've spoilt all the soft, pretty colours. Why it's nothing now, it just looks like a lump of raspberry jam. Why have you done it, Gabriele?" cried Miss Dolly. But little Johnnie gave no answer, he had run from the room.

Significant Experience

"I SUPPOSE" said Chris Loveridge "that no people understand these matters as well as the French" and since his fellow firewatchers were quite unable to escape from his company, they supposed so too.

"They are" he went on "the only really adult race. They have none of the Anglo-Saxon's lunatic notion that it is somehow sinful or disgraceful to learn love-making as one would any other art. Any boy of good family is expected to take a mistress by the time he is eighteen and these women have a respected place in society. They are often, clever, talented women, and they regard their job of instructing young men in the art of love-making with proper seriousness. The experience a young man may have with an older woman in this way is often highly significant".

Jeremy wondered how many more such evenings they would have to endure before a wisely directed bomb removed Chris Loveridge from their midst. Experience with an older woman, indeed; he wondered what Loveridge would do if he told him the story of his affaire with Prue in the summer of 1936; and yet, in a way, it *had* been significant.

It was so cool inside the patisserie that Jeremy would gladly have stayed on there for ever. Every afternoon of his holiday he had sat there while Prue was "lying down" at the hotel, and it was therefore the one ritual of the days together that had not been scarred by her growing

L

possessiveness, her "scenes", her engulfing unhappiness. He loved the little shop with its beaded curtains shutting off the glare of the sun, the bottles with their Dana Gibson figures filled with pink and white and mauve dragées. At twenty-two he still had much of the schoolboy's appetite and could happily consume unlimited quantities of marron glacés and raspberry water-ices. He was filled with elation as he repeated to himself "To-morrow she and I will separate. To-morrow I will be alone". To think that he had been jealous of Kuno, jealous of his deeper hold on Prue, had hated him for living on Prue's money—now he was only grateful to this German gigolo whom he had never seen for sending the telegrams that were taking her north to Paris. He only felt afraid that his resolution to let her go would weaken in these last hours—evaporate in the pleasure that her charm and beauty could still provide, dissolve before the pity that her tears could inspire. To-morrow he would be freed from this struggle, but if only meanwhile he could just sit here in the cool, with his fingers crossed against all dangers.

But Prue had denied herself her usual luminal sleep in order to spend with him what really was the last of their endless "last few afternoons together"; her head ached violently. To have sat on in the quiet and cool of the little shop would have offered her no martyr's crown, so they paid the patronne's daughter with the goitrous neck and emerged into the scorching heat of the afternoon sun.

"Let's explore the town" cried Prue, and when Jeremy demurred—"You really are the most horrifyingly uncurious person that ever lived, my sweet" she said. "We've been here a whole fortnight and we know nothing but the hotel, the plage and the port. You were born with the soul of a flaneur". Jeremy made no reply.

They turned into a side street that led out of the little town, treading carefully between decayed vegetables and rotting offal, which a large mongrel dog was tearing to pieces. There appeared to be no drainage, and dirty water ran between the cobblestones of the roadway. Now and again Jeremy was forced to retch as clouds of gaseous stench overcame him. The heat combined with the smell to increase Prue's headache, but she was determined not to show her rising ill-temper and Jeremy could but guess at the anger behind her sunglasses, the fury shaded by the broad brim of her beach hat; only at intervals when he spat into his handkerchief did she wince visibly. Suddenly in her determination to appear impassive she gazed too fixedly ahead and trod disastrously in a pool of muddy water, which seeped steadily under her sandal, wetting the sole of her foot and covering her scarlet toenails with mud. "God blast everything" she shouted, and then turning on Jeremy "If you had anything of a normal man's instincts you'd have known this wasn't the right direction." "Don't worry, duckie" said Jeremy "It couldn't matter less", but alarmed that he might have said the wrong thing, he suggested that she should remove her sandal and wipe her foot with his handkerchief. Prue did not reply.

If battle was joined in Jeremy's mind, Armageddon was being fought within Prue's. She knew that she could not let Kuno turn to some other woman to pay his debts, could not give up the habit of life with him, yet these few weeks had not been long enough to free her from her wild desire for Jeremy. To know that she must leave him and that he welcomed her going made her long to hurt him, to put terror into those round calf's eyes, to see those boyish features wince. She knew her own moods so well, could detect already the pattern of physical discomfort, nervous tension, apparently just occurring, yet in reality contrived by herself, that would end in a violent outburst. She anticipated his misery answering her violence, and her own pleasure as she watched unhappiness cloud his face. Finally she foresaw her own agonies of remorse and self-abasement that would end the cycle. Her whole soul revolted from it. Oh God let me leave at least *one* of these boys with happy memories of me, she thought.

Now they left the town along a glaring road of hard, white stones. Jeremy gazed with relief to the left where the dark lines of the olive trees, broken here and there by a crumbling grey wall, stretched far away into the disorder and savagery of the mountains. Prue walked on silently, with set features, occasionally kicking her foot against the road surface to dislodge stones that were pressed into the fragile soles of her sandals. Every now and again she would stop and move her mouth as though to speak, but nothing was said. Jeremy knew that she was holding herself back from one of those conversations ending in rows which she knew so well how to contrive, and he tried to assist her resolution.

"I should like to be here when the broom is in flower" he said.

"Yes" said Prue "that would be nice. Perhaps we could come together next spring. But, of course I forgot" she added bitterly "1937 is a very special year for you, a year in which you'll be doing all sorts of important things with your life".

Jeremy would not compromise on this, would make no promises however vague on which she could build false hopes, so they walked on in a tense silence. He looked to the right at the small bourgeois villas with their hybiscus hedges. Then for a time he could see nothing but the tops of the fig trees above the long white convent wall. Suddenly they came upon a villa garden more ornate than the rest with a fountain and oleander trees, their flowers as sugary a pink and white as the dragées in the tea shop. In front of the white villa itself were beds of cannas and of zinnias, and a large ornamental clock composed of begonias and rock cabbages. All the flowers looked faded and dry in the heat, their petals and leaves covered in dust. On the verandah was seated an old, old woman in a black dress and she too looked dried up and dusty. The whole deadened spectacle connected in his mind with his thoughts about Prue and he shuddered.

"There's something quite horrifying to me in exposing the moribund to the public view" he said. "That old woman ought to be in her grave by now with a respectable glass case of immortelles and a coloured photograph as her sole memorials".

"Don't you *ever* find people a bloody bore?" snapped Prue, then she added "Books and people and talk, books and people and talk, that's all life means to you. I sometimes wonder if you'll ever *do* anything with your life." "I don't think there's any fear of that now. You've taught me what fun doing can be, duckie" he said, and prayed God that one such statement would suffice for her.

Prue's grey eyes came alive with pleasure and she pressed the backs of her fingers against his cheek. "You're an awful sweety pie" she said.

"I thought you'd like me to say it" said Jeremy and he tried to cover up the bitterness in his voice with one of the sidelong looks she so adored, but all to no avail.

"You can also be a bloody little cad" she said in a hard drawl. "My God! when I think what I would do if *I* was twenty-two again, with all your chances in life". Jeremy made no reply, the six weeks had at least taught him the sincerity of her hatred of being thirty-five. He felt intensely sorry for her, wished so much that he could help. Whatever the dismal wreckage events had made of their passion, he could still remember so clearly her gaiety, her beauty, the wonderful variety in life that she had revealed to him when he had first met her in Paris only six weeks earlier. If he could have given her some hope for her future it would have been different, but he knew now how impossible that was. No sooner were the fragments of her life welded together than disintegration began again, sometimes in slow gradual decay, sometimes bursting apart when the splendour of the vessel seemed most bright, always broken by her own fears, by her own insecurity, as she held on to everything she possessed with a tighter and tighter grip until it was smashed to pieces. She would drink to retain her gaiety and wit, drug to secure her sleep, deny herself for fear of losing her money and then waste it for fear of losing what it could give, and above all she must possess her lovers and her friends until she had destroyed herself or them. All he could hope to do for her was to make this last day together a happy one, to stifle his feverish relief as he thought of the future, to bury his bitterness as he contemplated the waste of the past. For himself he knew that he must get away if he was not to be devitalized, must pit his own direct will to live and his youthful vitality against her hysteric attacks, her sick will to hold him.

"It's funny" Prue's voice broke in on his thoughts "when I was young and was surrounded by nothing but foxhunting farmers and young naval lieutenants I used to long to know someone, some man who was clever and sensitive. I imagined that poets and artists, yes and even actors, must lead the most wonderful lives, creative, important. Well I've met them now. Christ! What a procession. Wasters, spongers, frauds, perverts, I've known the whole bloody circus. Yes, and been their adoring mother to go to bed with and tell their little dreams to. Plenty of those, dreams of all sizes, going to be this, going to write that. 'Be my inspiration, let me lay my head in your lap', and then always the same little squeal 'You're getting in the way of my schemes. I'm a creative artist, I'm above human affections'. All of them going somewhere important, so will dear Prue please pay the fare? Prue paid all right and where the hell have they got to in their dear little dream boats? Roger a fifth rate dress designer, Tony a sot in Capri, Bernard on tour in revue...."

Not that category again, thought Jeremy, at all costs he must stop that. He took her hand and held it.

"Don't let Kuno get under your skin" he said "If he's that bad, get rid of him".

Prue wrenched her hand away and began to shout at him. "You'd better pipe down about Kuno" she cried "He has at least got some sense of responsibility—He knows what he wants and he gets it."

"He's certainly got you alright" said Jeremy. "It's a curious thing" replied Prue "with really dishonest people like you. They always love to harp upon other people's money motives. Do you really think it matters a damn to me that I pay Kuno, at least I know it's within my income. The price I pay for unbought love like yours is far too high, there's such a thing as being bored to death, you know".

Jeremy thought of his own wasted vacation, the books unread, the places unseen, even the failure to acquire spoken French, but he was determined not to prolong the scene so he merely smiled at her. "We've both said far too much for one afternoon" he mumbled.

"My God you're right" Prue shouted "I don't think I want to hear any more talk for the rest of time". It's true, she thought, he does bore me, I've heard it all before so often—the young idea. Well, why the hell go on with it? she asked herself, the seduction's over, duckie, the bedroom scene's through, clear out. But immediately she realized that without Kuno to go to, she would have hung on to Jeremy as she had to all the others, as she must hang on so long as Adonis kept one look of virginity for her still to outrage. Thank God for Kuno then with his debts, his sponging, his violent jealousy and his rages. There would be plenty of them all when she got back to Paris, visits to lawyers, talks with tradesmen, searching his suits to get the story straight, the furniture flying about—no possibility of Jeremy when Kuno was around, but for all that she would be glad to get back to the old gossip, the old round of bars, to Kuno's expertise. Or would she? My God, she thought what a bloody fool I was to stage the big exit from home; but it was all broken up now—her mother in a hotel at Cheltenham, Eve married to a major in Simla. The convent days had been her only happy ones, with Sister Anne Marie and the Reverend Mother. Prudence Armitage had been one of their prize pupils.

"God knows how you Protestants can be expected to have any sense of direction" she said. "It's different with us, I haven't been to mass for years, I've got every mortal sin on my conscience, but I know when I'm doing wrong. I'm still a Catholic, it's there, nothing can take it away from me".

"Of course, duckie" said Jeremy who had met this mood so often now "once a Catholic always a Catholic" and he reflected with satisfaction that that particular act would probably not have to be repeated before they parted.

The road had begun to narrow now and suddenly they found themselves in a small farmyard. Some meagre brown hens, with here and there a bantam, were scratching in the dust. Guinea fowl gleamed black and white against the shining leaves of the figtree in which they roosted, their pinheads with their scarlet eyes trembling and nodding like those of palsied old women. At the sound of intruders they let forth their raucous screams, turning the farmyard to jungle. Two large dogs came out from a barn and began to run towards Prue and Jeremy, barking wildly. Jeremy threw some stones at them. "Away Cerberus" he said, and to Prue "We'd better retrace our steps".

The restorative effect of a luxurious bathroom upon jaded nerves is astonishing; both Prue and Jeremy faced each other with genuine pleasure across their table on the hotel terrace. Almost immediately beneath them the rocks ran down to a deep clear sea, still blue, but darkening with the evening sky. Away across the bay the bright red cliffs were changing to a sombre brown; far inland as it seemed they could see the yachts jostling and crowding each other in the harbour, whilst here and there a brightly coloured light began to shine forth reminding them of the approaching Quatorze Juillet festival. Here at the end of the cape they seemed far out at sea, isolated from the world, but there was no sense of loneliness.

Jeremy had ordered champagne and Prue's evident delight at the tribute gave him great pleasure.

"Poisson du golfe again, duckie" he said "oh! the

fishbones that litter these shores. Gott sei Dank it's not that awful bouillabaise. The horror of that saffron. I shall never praise crocuses again as long as I live."

"I'm so hungry I could eat anything" said Prue "Even the eternal gulf fish". Looking at him with his black hair running in points from his ears, his look of a little boy playing the homme du monde, she knew where her appetite came from.

"Oh! Prue, only you could think of saying gulf fish. It's lovely, so distinguished, like Gulf Stream".

Really, he decided, she was extremely lovely with her straight green gold hair, large grey eyes and full sensual mouth. The excitement he had known when he first saw that soignée head came back to him. Diana huntress fair but no longer chaste, he had thought, and when he had known of her Irish girlhood and her later life of boites and lokals the mystery had been solved.

"I'm more than halfway through the 'Awkward Age'" said Prue. "You're quite right about how good it is. For the uneducated like myself it's so much easier than the longer ones, tho' I'm sure you're right about 'The Ambassadors' too if I could only have finished it. But I know all the people in the 'Awkward Age' so well, there are hundreds of Vans among the Americans in Paris and Mrs. Brook of course is Georgia Wright to the life, and as for that terrible Aggie I once had a young art student to live with me, she looked like Heaven itself, but, my dear, that girl's mind".

"You see how hipped James was on innocence" said Jeremy "I must say I find the spectacle of the pure Nanda among all those ravening wolves and tarnished women very moving."

"Yes" replied Prue in a doubtful tone "if one didn't feel James enjoyed the spectacle so. Oh! I know he makes innocence the ultimate virtue, and destroying it the ultimate sin. But how he does love watching the sinners at work. Innocence by itself would leave him cold, but put it in the wolves' den and watch his mouth water". She spoke almost savagely—let James be the whipping boy for her own prurience.

Jeremy waved his hands in acquiescence "You're absolutely right, Prue" he said "We've got so many dons like that. Pimps with eunuchs' voices and black silk ribbons to their glasses. You should hear one of them say 'Heaven forbid that you *should* understand, my dear young lady' to some girl in Eights Week".

Prue laughed delightedly. The champagne, the langouste, the pine scented air, the lapping of the sea on the rocks below them were making of this dinner one of those unexpected, never to be forgotten hours of happiness that so often form the penultimate of a love affair.

"Yes, it's all those people and what goes with them that put me on your side against Franco" said Prue. Jeremy's face darkened, Prue put her hand on his "I know what you're thinking, pie" she said "You feel you've no right to talk about it unless you're out there fighting with them. I'm sure it's crazy of me and only because I don't understand the value of what you're doing at Oxford, but I wish you were. I think if you did join the International Brigade, I'd get out there somehow as a nurse or an ambulance driver".

"What about the Church" said Jeremy.

"Aren't there priests and all and good men too with the Basques?" said Prue, Irish in her excitement.

Jeremy pressed her hand; he felt very fond of her at that moment. His historical sense blurred by the champagne, he saw himself carried from the barricades,

Camille Desmoulins with a few published poems to survive him, and Prue bending over his stretcher, her grey
eyes earnest, her hand steady as a rock, a sort of Madame
Roland with a past. Into Prue's mind came a vision of
the Countess tending Cherubino, his fair white flesh torn
and bathed in his own blood. Their fingers entwined
more closely. It was such a *happy* evening.

They were both pleasantly drunk as they left the hotel,
holding hands and rubbing against each other as they
descended the hill. Jeremy was entranced by the rhyth-
mic highpitched buzzing of the cicadas and the regular,
deep croak of the bullfrogs. As they drew nearer to the
harbour the strains of one of the thousand indistinguish-
able French quick foxtrots became louder, predominantly
the noise of accordions piercing and receding in their
heads, occasionally also the wail of a saxophone throb-
bing in the pits of their stomachs.

"It's going to be rather hell, duckie" said Jeremy "that
awful French jazz".

"Well, at least it *is* gay, sweet" said Prue. "Not like
that terrible bogus American band at the hotel. I shall
never forget the playfulness of that man singing 'Qui a
peur du grand loup?'"

"But still they gave us *our* tune, darling" Jeremy said
sentimentally, and as they passed the unplanted square
with its surround of plane trees where the old men in
their blue shirts and straw hats and walrus moustaches
were chatting after the last game of bowls, he began to
croon

> *"Was it just a dream*
> *That joy supreme that came to us in the gloom?"*

And Prue answered with mock drama

> "*No, no it wasn't a dream*
> *It was love in bloom*".

They arrived in the little port just in time for the fire-
works and stood with their arms round each other to
watch the dark water with its reflections of coloured
lights—green, red, blue, orange—break into a thousand
golden ripples as the Roman candles and Catherine wheels
scattered and revolved above it. Then they craned their
heads until their necks were stiff watching the rockets
explode their green and red meteors against the star
clustered sky. Finally there was the set piece with a great
Bastille outlined in amber burning to the ground and
then the singing of the Marseillaise. After that they
joined in the dancing on the hard concrete square,
packed closely, jogging up and down to the quick foxes,
swaying to the slow. Sometimes Prue would dance with
her arms hanging at her side, feeling Jeremy's movements with her body, at others she would hold him
closely, her thighs pressed against his. Soon they were
changing partners; a constantly varied blur of faces passed
in front of Jeremy, so that with the pernods and the coin-
treaus he took at the little café, the babble of voices and
the heat of human bodies, he began to feel queasy and the
concrete floor threatened to come up and strike him.
He took refuge at a little table with the mistress of a
Russian painter they had met during their stay. She was a
young cockney girl and her homely sophistication made
him feel sentimental for London. Prue was dancing
somewhat erotically with a very young French workman,
and every so often Jeremy could hear her voice and her
high hysterical laugh pitched rather above the general

din; her fair hair was falling in wisps and her head was surmounted by a red cardboard crown. Now and again as she passed near she would throw a streamer or some coloured balls at him. Jeremy could see that she was growing jealous, but he was not in the mood to care and he talked animatedly to the cockney girl. Nevertheless, when Prue came up to their table he thought it kinder to placate her. "Thank God you've come, darling" he said. "A French sailor's been bullying me to dance with him". He had gauged rightly, for all Prue's anger vanished in her excitement as she replied "Poor sweet they can't leave you alone, can they? Though you do look madly tapette when you're drunk, you know".

Jeremy laid his head back on the pillow and tried to think of something to say that would mend the situation, but it was useless. He felt angry with himself for not having given her a final "good time", since she set such store by these things. Circumstances had been so against him. Despite all Prue's teaching, he was still inexpert and drink only made him more clumsy; whilst she seemed to lose all restraint when drunk, and abandon that would have been attractive in a young girl only underlined her age and brought out all his suppressed prudery. This time, particularly, his mind had refused to act in co-ordination with his body, his thoughts leaped forward all the time to the future, to his freedom—he would visit Aigues Mortes and Montpellier, wander up through Arles and Nîmes, perhaps see the Burgundian tombs at Auxerre, he would read the new Montherlant he had bought in Paris, he might even write some poems again. He could hear her voice now behind his thoughts, complaining, scolding. Suddenly it came to him loudly, almost in a scream.

"You bloody little cad" she said. "Can't you even have the courtesy to listen to me?"

"I am listening, Prue, only I'm very tired, darling. You were saying that it wasn't a very happy ending to our relationship, but does the ending matter so very much?"

Prue's eyes narrowed. "You think you've got rid of me very easily don't you?" she said through half-closed teeth. "Did you really imagine that I was going to-morrow?" she said with a hysterical laugh. "Just because you've had all you want out of me, I'm to get out". Jeremy saw the scene breaking upon him that he had dreaded all day and he felt no energy to withstand it. "Don't talk so, darling" he said "We've been so happy. And there will be other times too in the future" he added weakly. Prue laughed again wildly "Oh yes" she cried "there'll be other times alright. Tomorrow, and the next day and the day after, because you see, you're not going to leave me" Jeremy's patience seemed to snap. "No, Prue, that's where you're wrong. You've got Kuno, and I've got something more important in life". Prue's face became contorted with fury, losing all control, she began hitting him wildly, pummelling his chest, biting his fingers and his chest, pulling his hair. Jeremy, however, knew his superior strength, holding her wrists tightly, he forced her head back on to the pillow. He felt a mounting desire to hurt her, bending over her he kissed her mouth savagely. "I'm kissing you because you're attractive" he laughed bitterly "but I'm going to leave you because you're such a bitch." Springing away from the bed, he began hurriedly to put on his dressing gown; but Prue was after him in a second, clawing and tearing at his hands with her long fingers. "*You*'re not going to leave me. Oh! no. Oh! no." Her voice was like that of a sarcastic schoolmistress. She was playing her last card with the threat of a public scene, but Jeremy's anger made him able to counter this move. With his left hand he smacked her across the face methodically and hard, with his right hand he twisted the arm that was clawing at him until the pain made her relax her grip and she sank, sobbing, on to the floor. As she looked up at him she saw that his mouth was bleeding. "My God I've hurt you" she cried. "Don't come near me, leave me alone. My God! how could I do it?" Jeremy knew this succeeding mood well also. Reassuring and pacifying her, he got her at last to bed. "We can't let this happen again, it's too degrading" she was still sobbing as she laid her head back "I must leave early tomorrow. We must not see each other again". But Jeremy felt no security in her moods any more. He saw clearly that to get free he must run away. "Here drink this off, duckie" he said, as he crushed up an extra luminal tablet. It was essential for his get-away that she should sleep late the next morning.

It was still only ten o'clock when Jeremy descended the imposing steps of Marseilles station and passed down the dusty sidepath between the stunted plane trees that flank the top end of the Canebière. He had over an hour to wait before the autobus which was to take him to Aigues Mortes, so, leaving his suitcase at the bus office, he bought some figs and peaches from a nearby stall, manoeuvred a complicated crossing of the tramway and sat at a table in one of the cafés at the lower end of the great street. Despite the alka seltzers he had taken that morning, his legs still wobbled beneath him and his head became confused when he bent down. He decided on a plain melon water ice, but then, overcome by greed, added a praliné cream ice to the order. In his jade green linen shirt, white silk scarf with green spots and olive green daks, he looked very English intellectual, very Pirates of Penzance.

He took out the Montherlant and began to read, but his attention wandered. The day was still cool and there was a light breeze, but there were already signs of the approaching heat in the hazy atmosphere rising from the pavements and in sudden warm gusts of wind. His heart was full of happiness at his new found freedom and his thoughts, as on the night before, were bent towards the future, but his nerves were still jarred at the tension of his last scene with Prue, he could not free his mind from the sense of imprisonment, which seemed almost stronger now that it was at an end, he still dreaded hearing her voice raised in pursuit of him, he was still turning their relationship over and over in his mind imagining her future life, coping with her problems, extricating himself from them, though his reason told him they no longer concerned him. Above all he was still filled with shame as he thought of her huddled on the floor tearing and clawing at him. He must have relaxation before he could concentrate on the future, must be released from the superstitious fear that her moods could effect him now that he had left her.

For a time he sat watching the populous street, the evanescent patterns of colours and shapes. At first he noticed only the orange and white of a young girl's dress, the butcher blue of a workman's trousers, the scarlet pompom on a sailor's cap. Then he saw more directly the shape and figures of the people passing, the children with their graceful forms and their shy oncoming eyes,

M

the developed figures of the young, their insolent sex-conscious walk and their bold eyes, the fat, the flabbiness of the middle-aged, the bent bodies and gnarled, wrinkled skins of the old—the pattern of Mediterranean life began to emerge. Now he could take in particular groups—the policeman's argument with a tram driver that grew into a crowd of gesticulating, shouting onlookers, the occasional Anglo Indian returning to England stopped by the Arab carpet merchant or the strawhatted, over-toothed tout, the jostling group of bourgeoises buying from the outside stalls of the Bon Marché. He decided to give himself a new tie and walked over to the stalls. It was while he was examining a tie of white crêpe-de-chine with scarlet spots that suddenly he felt a sharp nip in the fleshy part of his thigh. He turned quickly to see what had happened, but whoever was taking such a liberty—and he laughed to himself as the phrase came to his mind—had vanished in the throng of shoppers. The tie was altogether too chichi, he decided, and put it down. A moment later he felt a sharp pinch on the other thigh. As he turned round quickly he thought he saw a pair of laughing dark eyes disappear behind a stout peroxide-haired woman in an open work blouse. He moved rapidly towards the spot where his assailant had appeared, but only succeeded in jabbing the stout woman's breast with his elbow, and she began to expostulate violently. He decided to walk up the street towards his bus. By this time the Canebière was filled with people and he had con-siderable difficulty in moving rapidly through the crowd. He had only proceeded a few steps when the pinching began again, but now it was not only his thighs that were pinched, there were unmistakable and very painful nips in his fleshy buttocks. He dodged hastily round a tall negro soldier, almost knocking him over and being cursed as he made his getaway. Looking back, he now saw his assailant clearly, indeed he or she, for it was impossible to be sure of the sex, made no effort at concealment. It was a little child of about eleven years, dressed in a ragged shirt or blouse, and a pair of torn khaki cotton shorts; the child was indescribably dirty, with bare scabbed legs, the head was almost shaven, and the little face was strangely yellow and flat, but the eyes were dark and intensely alive, mischievous, almost, Jeremy thought, sexy. It began to sing in a high voice a gay little song, laughing and pointing at Jeremy, who felt certain that the words were personal if not obscene from the smiles of some passers by, though no one actually interfered. He began to walk more quickly, but the song still sounded in his ears, and soon the painful pinching was renewed. He turned sharply once or twice attempting to catch hold of the child or at least to hit it, but it was always too quick for him. Soon Jeremy found himself breaking into a run, the blood mounting to his cheeks with shame, as he dodged the ubiquitous child. The whole spectacle must seem incredibly absurd, like some ridiculous game of tig. The singing persisted, broken by occasional derisive shouts could it be in Arabic? he thought, but, no, it must be some Marseilles argot. At last he reached the bus office and took refuge in its cool depths for a few minutes. When he emerged the child had vanished, but as soon as he was seated in the bus he heard the infuriating song again—there, outside on the pavement was the beastly creature dancing up and down, pointing and laughing. He pretended to be buried in the Montherlant, but as the bus filled up with passengers he became more and more self-conscious. One or two people looked at him curiously, but no one said anything. The window was half open and he rested his hand for a moment on

the ledge, only to receive a sharp tap on the knuckles
from the creature outside who broke into cartwheels
with pleasure. A girl in the bus laughed openly, but
her mother checked her with a "Tais-toi, Ernestine" and
she subsided into handkerchief-suppressed giggles. At
last the bus moved off and Jeremy buried his
crimson face in his book, but as they sped along,
the tension, the embarrassment, the shame of the
incident left him and he became absorbed in the
new scenery through which he was passing. With
this immediate crushing misery and embarrassment
the whole burden of his life with Prue seemed
to pass from him, leaving him ready and eager for a
new life.

Dinner at the George had been a great success and all
four of them were feeling in gay but sentimental mood
when they returned to Jeremy's rooms. He dispensed
liberal glasses of port and then sat with one leg tucked
under him in the window seat. The others were laughing
and talking and playing Tino Rossi and Mae West
records, but he felt curiously silent and thoughtful. He
was pleased with the appearance of his room, the low
bookcases around the walls were a great improvement on
those provided by the college, the great green-white
chrysanthemums looked very chaste, the hard jade green
coarse woven cushions gave the required note of colour.
He would dearly have loved to strike a more modern note
with some of the Regency furniture he had seen in
London, but it was beyond his means. The glory of the
room, however, lay in the genuine Toulouse Lautrec
coloured lithograph of the Folies Bergeres which had
been his summer extravagance. He looked out over the

Fellows' garden to Christ Church meadow and the river where the October mists were already rising, everything seemed supremely peaceful and happy. He felt really interested in Vaughan and Herbert, his tutor was inspiring, he was College Secretary for Aid to Spain, he had been promised a good part in the one act plays at the end of term, he had even written some poems. The beginning of the Second Year was a good time.

His guests had reached the stage of recounting their erotic experiences. Alastair MacDougal said nothing, he lay back in an armchair his long dark face sneering slightly. For him there had been yachting in the Mediterranean and shooting in Scotland. He was engaged to be married to a Tatler beauty, there would be a Hanover Square wedding, that was all there was to it. The antics of the others were middle class, amusing, to be tolerated if you like, but always rather absurd. Jeremy wondered how long he would be tolerant after he had gone down, not long he imagined.

David looked so very Nordic as he reclined on the couch, resting in Valhalla, only his weak chin and petulant mouth spoiled the illusion. He was strumming on a mandoline and as they talked he would sing snatches of Schubertlieder in a rich if tremulous tenor. His story was one of seduction and he told it with a combination of sentiment and vanity that was most revealing—the doctor's elder daughter in love with him, her passion used as a cloak to seduce the more attractive, virginal younger sister. Jeremy remembered the bounderish rather pathetic major, David's father, cashiered for gambling, and as he listened he thought he knew what was in store for David.

In little Gerald Prescott, looking so very extra in his blue velvet tie and his West End stage haircut, it was easy to see the future touring actor. Gerald went depressingly according to type.

"Well, my dear, that's what they *told* me. Ask Jeremy he'll know. *Didn't* Tiberius do the most *frightful* things with children? Well *anyhow* Capri was *heaven*. *And* I met Bobbie Trundle. He's *madly* influential and knows every*one* and every*thing*. Of course I'd met him before but at Capri we got to know each other *really* well. He's *aw*fully charming, not frightfully young, of course, but *mad*ly distinguished looking. And, my dear, *does* he know his way about? We went down to Pompey when the fleet was in. . . ."

Yes, thought Jeremy, Gerald's future was all too clear. But what about himself? The future seemed to hold so many possibilities, so much that he might achieve, and of course so many dangers. He felt his chances were greater than those of the others, for at least he had fought one major battle and the victory had been his; and his mind turned to those blue, rough edged, thick papered letters from Paris, the first of which he had answered kindly but firmly, the last of which had remained unanswered and now they had ceased to arrive. How easy it was to feel certain that one had been right to act caddishly for once. Not the drifting caddishness of Gerald and David, but a constructive caddishness that made him feel justified in thinking that he was more interesting than the rest of his circle, less obvious and bourgeois.

"Jeremy's silence is most portentous" said David. "You haven't got married, have you?"

"Oh, my dear, *no*" said Gerald. "He'd look *much* more

miserable if that was the case.   Jeremy" he added, crouching on the floor and pointing his cigarette in its long holder at his host "You're *no* longer a virgin."

"Tell us all about her, dear boy" said David.   "If it was a she" said Gerald.

"I believe something really interesting may have happened to one of you at last" said Alastair, leaning forward in his chair.

Jeremy hesitated before telling them about Prue, for all their sophistication they seemed very young, they might so easily fail to see the point.

So "I did have rather a curious experience in Marseilles" he said.   He always enjoyed bewildering them and this time it was all quite true.

"*Marseilles*, my dear" said Gerald "It *couldn't* be more dangereux".

"Beware the pox, Jeremy, beware the pox" said David with weary wisdom.

"I think we might hear more about it" said Alastair, if he was prepared to sit with the mummers, he was not prepared to wait about for the performance to begin.

"It all happened with quite a young child" said Jeremy "with Murillo eyes".

"Really, dear boy" said David, all his prudery awakened.

"What sex of child may I ask?" said Gerald.

"You may ask" said Jeremy "but I can't answer".

"Was it a pleasant experience?" asked Alastair.

"Most painful while it lasted" said Jeremy "but the sense of relief when it was over was tremendous".

"I think all this mystification is in rather bad form" said David.   "You're a bit old, Jeremy, to try to épater les bourgeois in this way".

"I believe it was something rather important to Jeremy" said Alastair.

But Gerald too was rather nettled. "Oh! a *highly* significant experience, I'm sure" he said "Let's put on I'm No Angel. It's still *quite* my favourite Mae West number".

Mother's Sense of Fun

DONALD had awoken at six to hear those sounds of bustle and activity that he knew so well—quick scurryings that sounded like mice in the wainscotting, and hushed, penetrating whispers to Cook. There could be no doubt that his mother was up and about and that she intended to be particularly considerate to him after his journey. Over-long intimacy had invested each sound that she made with a particular significance, so that he soon recognized in the youthful jauntiness of her movements a pleasure in his return that went beyond her usual pride in being up so early. She was being especially thoughtful that he might have no cause for complaint, was laying up indulgence for herself, acquiring merit so that any independence he might claim would appear as ingratitude. No martyr could walk so bravely to her doom, as she to the stake she had built for herself.

Why should these household noises have such an accusing ring? He knew there were no duties that could not be performed later in the day, yet it seemed impossible to believe that in carrying them out so quietly his mother was not having to skimp them or expend extra energy upon them—and all this sacrifice of course was for him.

I am not equal to the fight, he thought bitterly. "The contest between Mrs. Carrington and her son for the prize of the latter's independence was an unsatisfactory one to the spectators, for the fight was very unequal. Mrs. Carrington, though a veteran in the ring, showed her old undiminished energy, whilst her punch seemed to have lost nothing of its force. Her speed and tactics were completely superior to those of her opponent, who seemed dazed and tired from the start. She sprang from one corner of the ring to another, seeming to be everywhere at once and dealing blows from the most unexpected angles". It was all so intensely unfair, he reflected, she had so many virtues and it was exactly those virtues which made life with her impossible. The crowd, too, was so often on her side, so often succumbed to her charm, all but his own few friends, those that she had not appropriated, and they, of course, were "impossible" people. "What a wonderful pal your mother must be" people would say to him "so easy going and alive and such a terrific sense of fun". It was of course absolutely true. At times she moved and even looked like a young girl, and she could then be a delightful companion, ready to go anywhere at any moment, and investing the most ordinary events with a sense of adventure. Despite her continuous anxieties and frets about household matters, she was ready to leave them aside at a moment's notice if she could share for a minute in his life. "I'm the mistress of the house" she would say "not the house of me". Since she rose at six and never retired before midnight she had, as she claimed, plenty of time to get things done. It was the other members of the household who suffered. Looking back, Donald realized that he could not remember leaving a theatre or an evening party without the sick apprehension that he would have to pass an hour or more before he was allowed to sink exhausted into bed. She always had a letter to write on which he could advise or something to finish off in the kitchen if he wouldn't mind giving a hand, or, in default of other employment, she could bustle about making a last cup of tea, which she would then bring to his bedside. "I really think this is my favourite moment of the day" she would say, sinking into the armchair "When we can both relax at last. What an extraordinary hat Olga had on. . . ." It was of course a nice Bohemian refusal to be dominated by routine, but it meant that they were both always a little overtired, always a little on edge.

As if to emphasize the underlying tension of his life at home, Mrs. Carrington's voice came floating towards him from the room outside, its cheerful metallic timbre striking a chill in him even as he lay in bed. "Nonsense, Cook" she was saying "You know very well you like standing in these queues. You take to them like a duck to water, they're just up your street". It was almost obscene, he decided, that one's mother should be so like a hospital nurse. It was difficult to decide which of her two voices more completely suggested the private ward. The sweet cooing which she used in moments of intimacy roused greater suspicion in him, for it called so openly for surrender. But his hostility was chiefly reserved for the high pitched jollity of her everyday speech, which, apart from being more aurally revolting, revealed her insensitive and bullying nature. All day long it seemed to shrill about the house in a constant stream of self-satisfied humour and obtuse commonsense. The words she employed, too, were surely specially designed to rob the English language of any pretensions to beauty it might possess. It was not exactly that she used outmoded slang like Miss Rutherford who was always "unable to care less" about things or to "like them more", or even the earlier slang of Aunt Nora with her "topholes" and "purple limits". He had often thought that to find his mother's phrases one would have to go to English translations of opera or the French and German prose books that he had used at school. It always "rained cats and dogs", that is if the rain did not "look like holding off"; Alice Stockfield "was a bit down in the mouth" but then she "let things get on top of her"; Roger Grant was "certainly no Adonis", but she had "an awfully soft spot in her heart for him". At the end of a tiring day he would often wait for one of these familiar phrases in an agony of apprehension that he feared to betray, for he knew that criticism would be met by wounded silence or the slow, crushing steamroller of her banter, the terrible levelling force of her sense of humour. She and Cook were having a "good old laugh" at that very moment. "Well I suppose we must have looked rather silly, ma'am" he could hear Cook saying. "Of course we did" his mother replied "You standing there with flour all over your face and me in that terrible old green dress and in front of us on the floor—a pudding. Didn't you notice his face? I've no doubt at all that when he got home to dinner that night at Surbiton or wherever inspectors of taxes live he told his wife that he'd seen a couple of lunatics —and of course we *are* completely crazy in this household".

The same cosy, family jokes, he thought, the same satisfaction with her own little world. The difficulty was that in attacking her in this way one felt so grossly unfair. If she had been some one else's mother one would have felt differently. She had an eye for the ridiculous that was all penetrating, and, in a great degree, that rarer quality, a sense of fun, so that he seldom went anywhere with her without having, what she so delighted in, "a good laugh". "That rare gift in a woman" Major Ashley had called it "the ability to laugh at herself". And it was quite true— on occasion she would even mock the very jargon in her speech which he criticized; "So I said to him in my

bright, jolly way" she would say. But the self-satis-
faction with which she laughed at herself, thought
Donald bitterly! There was never any real self-criticism
in her humour. No, the criticism was reserved for everything else—the ideas she could not understand, the
beauty she could not see, the feelings she could not
appreciate. Heaven preserve me from the laugh of a
really good woman, he said aloud.

As if to mock his mood the laughter and conversation
outside his room grew louder. It was clear that the period
of respite granted to him was approaching its end. Soon
she would fill the room with that proud sense of possession of which her early morning embrace was almost a
symbol. As he looked round the bedroom he realized
how much he hated it. The careful, dead good taste of its
furnishing bore the imprint of her withering hand. Yet
how much she delighted in emphasizing that it was *his*
room—"Donald's part of the world". She would be
longing to emphasize his return to it, waiting for him to
say how happy he was to be back there—well she would
have to say it for him. Nothing nauseated him more than
this pretence that he enjoyed a separate establishment.
It was a primary article of the household creed which she
reiterated every day that "civilized people could not live
on top of each other", "everyone must have his own
little place where he could do what he liked". As long as
he could remember she had fostered the belief in him
that his room was his private domain, only it would seem
to create stress by her constant invasion of it. The very
fiction of independence itself had been used as a weapon
against him, when as a boy he had resisted her claims—
"Remember, Donald" she had declared "I'm only a
visitor here and visitors should be treated with some
semblance of good manners".

At times he fancied the room as a battlefield littered with the skulls and skeletons of his past hopes. It brought before him a series of ever more dispiriting pictures—sick beds surrounded by cloying and fussy affection; nursery teas when his every private fantasy and ambition had been taken out, laughed at and put away with the nonsense knocked out of it; adolescent hours of study and dreams riddled through and through with nagging and banter and summons to petty errands: over twenty years now, of nauseating futility. Over these years there had grown up between him and his mother a thickly woven web of companionship and antipathy, and beneath that an inner web of love and hatred. As time passed the antipathy and hatred had grown paramount, as she gradually coiled round his life, breaking his moral fibre, softening and pulping so that at the last she could swallow him. "The Nightmare Life in Death is she" he quoted "that thicks man's blood with cold".

The kiss with which his mother greeted him as she brought in the breakfast tray was brisk and businesslike, the sting lay in the gesture with which she followed it—the stroking and rumpling of his hair. The same routine had persisted since his thirteenth year, he could almost hear her say the words he had known so well in his schooldays "We're a bit too old for kisses now, aren't we darling? But we're still mummy's boy". This morning he could see that she was hungry for some demonstration of the affection she had missed during his six months' absence; well, as far as he was concerned it should be a struggle á l'outrance.

"I hope you're quite rested, darling" said Mrs. Carrington "because you'll have to nerve yourself for a heart to heart with Cook. Only wild horses or a fond mother's love could have prevented her from waking you up hours ago". Donald made no answer, but lay back with his head on the pillow and his eyes closed, he was determined to show no sign of appreciation, determined to express no pleasure at being home once more. He watched his mother as she moved quietly but briskly about, settling his clothes and books with the businesslike reverence of a modern Martha. A ray of sunshine from the window picked out her neat grey shingled head—she had always refused to succumb to the more fashionable bleached hair, for she felt that white gave such a hard line to the face— outlined the bright, birdlike features with their pastel colouring of powder and faint rouge upon the cheeks— lipstick was all right for young girls, she would say, but not for old women like her. She looked like a robin, he decided, that had come in for warmth from the Christmas card snow scene outside as she hopped from object to object, folding her son's ties, rearranging the Christmas roses in the pewter mug on the mantelpiece; her bright quizzical eyes and her jolly little smile, her well cut grey woollen costume and her crimson silk blouse all helped to enhance the picture. "Look", she seemed to say, "I'm really rather wonderful for fifty-eight, so cheerful, almost 'cheeky', or course life hasn't been easy and it's taken a lot of pluck to keep going," and then if you liked robins on Christmas cards you would be filled with the requisite warmth towards her, would surrender to the appeal for protection and make a place for her by your fireside.

And if you did, he thought, you would be lost. No, it was on quite other things that you must concentrate if you were to save your soul alive. The brave humorous little smile was there, but the underlip stuck out in a discontented babyish pout, the blue eyes shone brightly but they shone with the hard light of egotism; above all the lines that ran down from her cheeks were lines of self-pity. It was true that he had left the liner at Southampton yesterday with mixed feelings, but he had not guessed how soon the old misery would descend upon him. It had only taken one evening in her company to realize what "home" and "mother" meant to him, shades of the prison house had indeed begun to close around the growing boy, and the horror of it was, he reflected, that it was not even as if he was a growing boy, he was twenty-five, an old "lag". The six months lecture tour in America had been his first escape since University days. When he was over there it had seemed as though he was free at last, but of course he had really only been a ticket of leave man. America, in any case, was a thing of the past,—that she had made clear to him in their conversation of the night before. "Well" she had said with half humorous patronage "they seem to be very much like other foreigners. Perfectly easy to get on with, so long as you remember that you are dealing with children. They don't sound as sensible as the French, but at any rate they're not so pompous as the Germans. Quite frankly I'm afraid the trouble with them is that they're all really rather common". It wasn't a period of his life she had shared in and the sooner it was forgotten the better. She had not done with the subject, he noticed, as he tried not to hear the comments she made whilst tidying his clothes.

"I hope you like the Christmas roses, I had almost to sell the family diamonds to buy them, but there, I'm forgetting they're probably two a penny in New York". "You don't imagine you're going to *wear* this terrible American tie, do you, darling? Unless you intend to take me to a guest night at the Ancient Order of Buffaloes. Somehow I don't think we'd fit in very well". "Gracious! how old-fashioned they must be over there, all those

naked girls on magazine covers! Why it's just the sort of
thing your great Uncle Tom used to hide in the desk in the
billiard room". God! why must she protract the agony
like this? thought Donald. If she wanted to remove his
self reliance from him, let her wheel him into the operat-
ing theatre and get it over with, let him at least be spared
this bright sick room talk, these preliminary flashes of the
surgeon's scalpel. At last Mrs. Carrington herself grew
impatient of skirmishing—"Your room hasn't changed
much, darling, has it?" she asked in a voice yearning for
affection. "The room hasn't changed at all" he answered
flatly, and as he said it he was sucked down by tiredness
at the truth of the statement. Nothing had changed, all
the illusions he had built up in his absence, all his beliefs
in new powers of defence faded before the persistence of
her attack. He could see before him the outline of the
coming week—the week of holiday before returning to
the office on which he had counted so much as a prepara-
tion for a new life of independence. There would be
successes for her when boring relatives came to the house,
when they visited Aunt Nora at Richmond or when she
showed off his tricks before friends she had made in his
absence; there would be Pyrrhic victories for him when
his friends came to the house and she gently but humorously
put them out of their ease; there would be truces when he
shopped with her at Harrod's, lunched with her at her club
or accompanied her to the family solicitor; there would
undoubtedly be at least one major conflict with loss of
temper and tears and sulking; and, at last, he would return
to work, broken in and trained to carry on life at home.

Some weeks later, Donald lay back in bed, luxuriating
in the pleasure of a sleep already closing upon him at the

N

early hour of half past ten. How strangely exact his fore-
cast of that week had been, save for one major event!
Yes, he thought, one must still call it a major event,
though perhaps in a few months or even weeks, it would
no longer be "major", for one must recognize the strange
tricks of human memory and affection—not that he would
have called himself cynical, only that time had taught him
to be a realist. Yes, it had been a most typical week,
almost a symbol of his whole relationship with his
mother.

First there had been the meeting with Alec. How she
must have resented his imposing Alec upon her in that
first week at home. How typical of his own subservience,
he reflected bitterly, that he had told her of meeting his
friend at all. There were certain of his friends of whom
she had never approved and Alec Lovat was one of them.
A clever Scottish Secondary school boy was not the sort
of Cambridge friend she had imagined for him, and their
common literary enthusiasms, in which she could not
share, did not improve the situation. She had been so
very eager to make this shy and angular youth feel at
home, but his lack of response had not been encouraging;
he persisted in remaining her son's friend and not hers.
He recalled the little frown of displeasure with which she
had heard of the meeting. "Alec!" she had said "well,
that *is* jolly. I expect he's changed a lot, the army's probably knocked most of the corners off him. He could be
so nice when he forgot for a moment that he'd worked
his way up from the bottom. He was so very proud of his
childish opinions and so very ashamed of his delightful
Scots accent".

"The Scots accent's quite disappeared now" he had
told her. "Gracious me" she had said "then he must
certainly be laughed back into it".

When the telephone rang that evening she had run to answer it. "But, of course, you must come" he had heard her say, and a moment later "Och! but what ha'e ye done wi' your gude Scots tongue? I hope ye no ha'e left it in Eetaly".

She had chosen to invite a young French girl to meet Alec at dinner. She had a great liking for the dead conventionality and empty chic of French middle class women and this girl had been a superb specimen of her kind. The evening had not been a success. Poor Alec's shyness had only vanished for a moment when he began to speak of his new-found enthusiasm for the Early Wordsworth. "It's all nonsense" he had said excitedly "to expect the Prelude without that first attempt at a new freshness. Some of it's absurd if you like. . . ." "Now you're very naughty, Alec" broke in Mrs. Carrington "*I* know you're only pulling our legs, but gracious me, you'll have Mademoiselle Planquet thinking you mean it. Remember the dignity you have to uphold as the first real live Professor of English she's ever met." When Alec protested his sincerity, she laughed a little and then said abruptly "Fiddlesticks, why I suppose you'll be telling me next that 'The Idiot Boy' is the finest poem in the English language. I expect just the same nonsense goes on in France, Mademoiselle Planquet. As soon as we've got one stuffy old writer put safely away in the cupboard, these ridiculous children have to fish him out and dust him up again. They haven't got enough to do, that's the trouble".

The Samuels' cocktail party, of course, had been asking for trouble, but his mother had insisted on going. If she disliked Alec Lovat, she hated Rosa Samuel. The Samuels were richer and more sophisticated than she was. But above everything she was jealous of Rosa. That innocent visit he had made to them in Essex in Summer 1942 had been the root of the trouble. "Rosa Samuel behaved very stupidly with Donald" she had told Aunt Nora.

Rosa, in her own words, "had gone all 1912". Her sleek, dark hair was piled up high on her head with some construction of scarlet fruit and feathers in it, and her scarlet velvet dress which spread out in a train round her ankles was cut up the side of its very tight skirt. Donald remembered that as she had come forward to greet them his heart had jumped with triumph, here at least he was on friendly soil, for Rosa had been his confidante and ally in all his battles. Almost immediately, however, he had felt sure that his mother would win. So, indeed, it had proved, for Rosa in her mingled shyness and dislike had foolishly set out to shock. She greeted them with a self-consciously amusing account of her return journey from Switzerland. It appeared that she had got into conversation with a young girl "with the face of the Little Flower, my dear", but it had soon become clear that the relations of the saintlike creature with her elderly uncle were not entirely conventional. "Apparently, duckie" Rosa had said in her deep yet strangulated voice "he makes her stand in nothing but her stockings and thrashes her with a cow hide whip. But the incredible thing was that she told me all the horrifying details in an offhand bored way, just as though she was describing a shopping expedition to the greengrocers." His mother had rocked with laughter. "Goodness gracious, Mrs. Samuel" she had said "it takes a really moral person like yourself to imagine that the lives of people like that *are* anything but very boring." "Old bitch" Rosa had said to him later in the evening "I know she was as shocked as hell, but you can never catch her out". His mother had not waited for her hostess to pass out of earshot before she had said to him "How it all reminds me of those Edwardian parties at Grandfather Carrington's down at Maidenhead. All this silly smoking room smut, they want a good smack on the behind".

"I can't help liking Rosa Samuel" she had said, as they made their way home afterwards "she's so very stupid, that it would really be impossible to *dis*like her. Someone ought to tell her about her clothes though, darling. Whatever *had* she got that ridiculous Christmas tree on her head for? and that scarlet dress! It was just like an early film of Pola Negri's. I kept on thinking she'd bring a secret message out of her bosom". He had tried, he remembered, to turn the conversation on to a young woman archaeologist whom he had met at the party and liked; *her* clothes, at least, had been of the simplest variety. His mother however had been quite equal to this, indeed there was nothing she liked better than to have things both ways. "I thought she was a very nice girl" she had said "It seemed such a pity that she had to wear those lumpy clothes and sensible shoes. You have to have such a very good complexion, too, to go without make-up like that. Anyone could see she was an intelligent person without all that parade. Dear me! they'll be wearing placards next with B.A.Oxon or whatever it is written on them". A mood of compromise had descended upon him. Let me betray anything, let me sacrifice Rosa, let me forswear my belief in intellectual standards, he had thought, only let me be at peace with her, let us agree. He happened to have overheard a pretentious conversation about the theatre between three people at the party, and this he had told her, knowing that in so doing he was feeding her with ammunition for future attacks on his "clever" friends. "I sometimes wonder if they know

themselves what they mean when they use this jargon"
he had said. "They were discussing a play, mother, and
Olive Vernon said she didn't like it although she thought
it was good theatre. 'Good theatre' said her husband
'I thought it was thundering bad theatre'. Then that
stupid Stokes boy broke in 'I really don't think it was
theatre at all, I mean you have to have some glitter if
you're going to have theatre and it was so drab'. 'Oh!
but that sort of drabness' said Olive in her silliest voice
'surely *is* just a kind of inverted glitter'." His mother had
been delighted with the story "They really *are* a pack of
ninnies" she had exclaimed.

How different she had been with Commander and Mrs.
Stokes who dined with them the following evening! The
Stokes, whom she had met during his absence, had
proved to be a dull and somewhat self-satisfied couple
and it had been clear from the start that they were to be a
kind of private joke between them. Whenever Mrs.
Stokes had said something unusually snobbish, his
mother had taken great delight in catching Donald's eye,
whilst, at the end of a particularly long story of the
Commander's about life aboard the *Nelson*, she had
smiled sweetly and said "Well, that's most interesting.
I feel as though I'd been afloat for years, don't you,
Donald?" After their guests had gone she had sat down
and roared with laughter. "You really are wicked,
Donald" she had cried "making me laugh at the poor
creatures like that. They'll never set the Thames on fire,
but still they're better than those silly intellectuals we met
at the Samuels. Ah! well, thank God for a sense of
humour, without it the evening might have been very
dull". How he had longed to say that even with it the
evening had not been very interesting.

Politics, of course, had come under discussion when

Uncle Ernest came to lunch. The open ruthlessness of his Uncle's particular brand of city conservatism always outraged his social conscience and they had soon been engaged in a heated argument. His mother had been so amusing at both their expenses. "You haven't given the Labour people a chance, Ernest" she had declared "They've had no time to do anything yet. Remember that it's all quite new to them. Most of them have been mayors or town councillors or some other dreadful smug thing and they're bound to be a bit dazed now they've got to *do* something. Why by this time next year they'll be as sound old Tories as even *you* could want".

The visit to Aunt Nora, of course, had brought the usual row with it. He flattered himself that he recognized the sense of duty and real kindness of heart that inspired these determined visits to that impoverished and irritating woman. It was true that Aunt Nora would have felt snubbed if they had not been to see her, but when he reflected that her silliness would lead his mother to say a hundred snubbing things before they had left "Rose Cottage", it was not surprising that he had always found these expeditions depressing and pointless.

It had been without eagerness, then, that he walked through Richmond Park towards Aunt Nora's house. The day, he remembered so vividly, had been sunny and cold and he had stood for a moment to gaze at the twisted grey elm trunks and their tracery of black boughs outlined against the sky. "It would be nice," he had said "to spend a day in the country before the holiday is over". "I dare say" his mother had replied "but that's no excuse for being late for Nora. You know how she looks forward to this visit". Suddenly the futility of the whole week had impressed itself upon him. "Damn Nora and damn you", he had shouted "I never do a bloody thing

I want to". "Really, Donald, that's ridiculous. The whole week's been given up to amusing you. In any case we sometimes have to do our duty, even though we don't like it". The calm commonsense of her reply had been more than he could bear. It was too unfair that she should always have her cake and eat it in this way, he had felt. He had let out at her where he knew it would hurt most. "Oh, for God's sake spare us your quotations from Samuel Smiles. I know all about your religion" he cried out "but the whole thing's meaningless. I don't believe you have any real *faith*, just a lot of sentiment and cherished illusions you've kept from your childhood". His mother had begun to cry, for, as he well knew, in attacking her religion he had dealt her a serious blow. She had a number of ethical principles and these she held firmly. She had also a certain private devotional life which centred round the prayerbook she had been given at her confirmation. He had looked into this book when he was younger and had found between its leaves some love letters from his father written during their engagement, that happy period of her life before the physical contact of marriage had come to awaken and shock her, when she lived in that state of emotional flirtation, which she had tried to recreate with him. Of real religious beliefs concerning God and immortality she was quite uncertain, and far too afraid of her doubts to probe further. In speaking so violently, he had attacked the secret citadel of her life and she had only been able to find refuge in tears.

In a sense it had been his only victory of the week for after it she had been most anxious to make amends. She had realized that she must have annoyed him very deeply to provoke him to such an attack. "My poor darling" she had said "you must certainly have your walk in the woods". They must go to his favourite Epping on the Friday she had announced.

Friday had proved to be a wet and dismal day but nothing would deter her from making the expedition. "Nonsense! the walk will do you good" she had said in answer to his protestations. They had been marooned in the Forest during a violent rainstorm and had been drenched to the skin. On Saturday she had woken with a bad cold, but had remained on her feet with a depressing and determined cheerfulness. That night she had complained of sharp pains in the chest and on the next day she had developed pneumonia. Was it unnatural, he wondered, to have felt so little about it. No, surely, things had gone too far between them for him to have felt anything but an ashamed relief. The fight she had put up had roused his pity and admiration, though. She was a tough little woman and she had a strong will to live, but she was, after all, fifty-eight, and Death had taken her all the same. She had only been conscious once during the last two days of her life and Donald had been at her bedside. He had hardly been able to recognize the little, thin, blue-grey face, or the vague, alarmed kitten's eyes, for she had known that she was dying and she had been very frightened. He had wished so much to comfort her, but he had only felt very, very tired. She had signed to him to bend down beside her and had run her hand feebly over his hair. "My poor boy" he had just been able to hear her murmur "My poor boy will be very lonely without Mother".

Yes, life had been very hectic after her death, Donald thought as he stretched his limbs sensuously. His days were his own now to do as he liked, though it was strange how difficult he found it to decide what to do with them. That was to be expected with a new found freedom, it was bound to take a little time, the main thing was that he was free. She had said that the walk in the Forest "would do him good", he thought sardonically,—poor Mother it was not really the sort of joke that she would have cared for. It was with a smile on his lips that he slipped into sleep. . . .

He was at a reception, many hundreds of people were there and he was talking animatedly. They were in a long, lofty room with great, high windows and heavy curtains; it appeared to be in some medieval castle. Gradually a storm blew up outside, the winds howled and the heavy curtains flapped about in the huge room, like enormous birds; it began to grow very dark. The other people in the room huddled together in close, little groups, but he was left standing alone. Soon the people began to fade away and it grew darker and darker. Somebody ought to be with him, he could not be left alone like this, somebody was not there who should have been there. He began to scream. He awoke with his face buried in the pillow and he felt dreadfully lonely, so lonely that he began to cry. He told himself that this sense of solitude would pass with time, but in his heart he knew that this was not true. He might be free in little things, but in essentials she had tied him to her and now she had left him for ever. She had had the last word in the matter as usual. "My poor boy will be lonely" she had said. She was dead right.

Et Dona Ferentes

"I'LL have a cigarette too, Mother" said Monica to Mrs. Rackham "it'll help to keep the midges off. That's why I always hate woods so. Oh don't worry, Elizabeth" she added as she saw her own daughter's look of alarm. "That's why I *hate* woods, but there are hundreds and hundreds of more important reasons why I *love* them—especially pine woods. To begin with there's the scent, and *you* can say what you like, Edwin" she smiled up at her husband, who was frowning as he cut inexpertly at a block of wood with a pocket knife "about its being a hackneyed smell. But apart from the scent, there's the effect of light and shade. The only time that you can really see the sunlight out of doors is when it shines through dark trees like these. When you're in it, you're always too hot or too dazzled to notice anything. So you see, darling" she turned again to her daughter "I *do* love pinewoods". For a moment she lay back, but the smoke from her cigarette got into her eyes and soon she was stubbing it out on the bed of pine-needles beneath. "How I *do* hate cigarettes" she cried "and how I *do* hate hating them. It puts one at such a social disadvantage. Oh! it's all right for you, Mother, everyone in your generation smoked, and *smoked* determinedly; and it's all right for Elizabeth, when she's eighteen—don't let's talk of it there's only two years—nobody will even think of smoking, it'll be so dowdy; but with women in the forties like me there was always that awful choice—to smoke or not to smoke—and I chose not to, and there I am of course on occasions like parties and things with nothing to do with my hands. Now let's all lie back and relax for a quarter of an hour" she went on and the nervous tension in her voice seemed even greater than before as she said it "and then we can have a drink before lunch. Don't you think it was clever of me to remember to bring gin? People *always* forget it on picnics and yet it's so lovely to be able to have a drink without needing to be jolly. I hope nobody is going to be jolly, by the way. I forbid anyone to be jolly", she said with mock sternness and then turning to her son who was watching a squirrel in a nearby tree "Richard, darling, take that knife away from your father before he does himself an injury".

"It wouldn't be a very serious injury, Mother, and then Elizabeth could show her prowess as a First Aider or whatever they're called in the Guides" said Richard, but nevertheless he moved slowly towards his father. Before he could offer assistance, however, a tall fair haired youth had sprung forward.

"Allow me, please, Mr. Newman" he said, the stiffness of his foreign English relieved by the charm and intimacy of his smile "I am very able to cut wood with these kind of knives".

"That's very kind of you, Sven" said Monica "there you are, darlings, you see, Sven has manners. I'm surprised you weren't able to learn a few, Richard, when you were staying with him in Sweden. I'm afraid we lost all our manners here while we were busy fighting the war".

Two sharp points of red glowed suddenly on the Swedish boy's high cheekbones and his already slanting eyes narrowed and blinked.

Edwin Newman glared angrily at his wife, his prominent Adam's apple jerking convulsively above his open-necked shirt. He placed a hand on Sven's shoulder.

"You have given us so many useful lessons since you arrived, Sven, if you use the same charm to re-educate us in everyday courtesy, we shall be fortunate" he said.

"You are too kind to say these many good things to me, Mr. Newman" replied the boy "I hope I shall not quite fail to deserve them".

"You two ought to be talking in Latin" said Richard "You sound like Dr. Johnson, Dad, when he met famous foreign scholars. By the way, Grannie, have you been getting at Sven about his reading? I can't persuade him to read anything decent like De Quincey or Dickens or Coleridge. He seems to think for some reason or other that he's got to wade through 'Rasselas' in order to 'appreciate literature' as he calls it. I must say I shouldn't have thought even you would have inflicted that torture upon anyone".

Mrs. Rackham's heavy square-jawed face lost its look of grimness for a moment as she spoke to her beloved grandson.

"I am delighted to hear of a blow being struck at this neo-romantic nonsense. Like Miss Deborah I think that nothing but good can arise from reading the works of the great Lexicographer. Continue to read Rasselas," she said to Sven "and you may yet know what the English language should really sound like. Take no notice of Richard's attempts to lure you into reading Dickens. He only wants you to fall under a railway train like a famous English retired officer, Captain Brown, whose unhealthy interest in Boz led him to that horrid end".

"That just shows how little you understand about it, Grannie. Captain Brown was reading Pickwick and Pickwick's nothing to do with the real Dickens. Anyhow it was Pickwick in weekly parts which couldn't happen now."

"Isn't it time you two stopped all this Who's Who in Literature" said Edwin, "In any case, if Sven's going to waste his time on novels surely he might read modern authors like Huxley or even Lawrence".

"Dear Edwin" replied Mrs. Rackham "Even I know that Huxley or even Lawrence" and she imitated her son-in-law's hesitant tones "daring though they may be are not *modern* authors".

"In any case I am reading Rasselas because it is demanded for the higher examination. I am not really so greatly interested to read books". Sven lay back and stretched his arms out to a spot where the sunlight had broken through "I think I prefer more to follow outdoor games when the sun shines, like Elizabeth does" and he smiled lazily towards the clearing where Elizabeth was staking little wooden sticks around a clump of late bluebells.

Seen upside down it's more like a cat's than a satyr's thought Edwin.

Elizabeth only scowled "This isn't an outdoor game" she said "I'm just messing around. Come down to the stream with me, Mummie" she called.

"May I come too?" said Mrs. Rackham. Elizabeth gave no answer, but Monica looked pleased and held out her hand to assist her mother from the ground. The family likeness showed clearly as they walked away— three generations—hand in hand.

"It's the most lovely stream, Mummie" said Elizabeth, squeezing Monica's arm. "I wish we had it all for our own".

"Yes" said Monica "I would plant Japanese irises here—the dark purple kind with the spear-like leaves to contrast with the yellow flags. It's funny how profuse Nature is with yellow, now if I had made the Universe I should have had much more contrast of colour and more subtlety too with wild flowers. I wonder if fritillary would grow here, the place could do with something a bit more strange".

"But Mummie, it would be awful to change it when it's so beautiful".

"I don't think so, darling" said Monica "I don't know, of course, but I've always thought that was a false sort of romanticism. I don't believe you really become aware of the beauty of a scene until you see how it could be made more beautiful. What do you think, Mother?"

Mrs. Rackham smiled. "I think I just see the stream and the meadows behind" she said "and then I feel a great sense of peace and solitude".

"Oh yes, that of course" cried her daughter "but there's something else too. You have to look at it properly surely to see the patterns of shape and colour and that's when you see what's needed to complete them". She thought for a moment, then added "Yes, I'm sure you have to do that, otherwise it's all a blur and you don't really see anything".

"Look, Mummie, those holes" cried Elizabeth "I think there must be badgers. If you were here at night you would see them come down to drink".

"I should like that" said Monica "When there was no moon—at dusk or dawn—with black water and those nightmare deformed willow-trees and then lumbering grey shapes coming down to drink. But not by moonlight, that would be too expected".

"We've been imagining the badgers drinking in the stream" said Elizabeth to her father when they returned.

"Is that one of Brock's nightly prowls?" asked Edwin.

"No, darling", replied Monica "*not* Brock and *not* nightly prowls. Just badgers drinking. There were rabbits, too, but they weren't wearing sky blue shorts, they were just brown rabbits with white tails". Then seeing her husband's hurt expression, she put her hand on his arm "Never mind, darling", she said "You like imagining in that whimsical way, I don't; but I think it's only because I don't know how to".

Edwin smiled "How about that gin you were talking about?" he asked.

"It's in the shaker, darling, with some French. You do the shaking, you're so professional".

Indeed with his boyish face and long black hair, dressed in a saxeblue Aertex shirt and navy blue Daks Edwin looked very much like some barman from a smart bar in Cannes or like some cabaret turn. He seemed almost to be guying the part as he waved the shaker to and fro, dancing up and down, and singing grotesquely "Hold that Tiger".

"Idiot" cried Monica, and, relenting further, she turned to Sven "Do respectable fathers of families ever behave so absurdly in Sweden?"

"I do not imagine Mr. Newman a father of a family, I imagine him to have continual youth".

Monica turned away sharply "At eighteen, of course, one can imagine so many ridiculous things" she said.

But Edwin ended his dance with a mock bow.

"The spirit of youth is infectious" he declared. Sven lay back and laughed with delight, showing his regular, white teeth.

It was while they were eating their lunch that Edwin got on to his hobby horse.

"There's supposed to be a Saxon camp across on that hill over there" he said, pointing to the East. "If my theory is right it may well be an example of a Saxon settlement existing alongside a British one".

He was so used to a completely silent audience that he was quite startled when Sven said "Can that really be?"

"I believe so, but it's a view which is only gradually gaining ground" said Edwin and he looked across at Sven who sat clasping his legs, with his knees up to his chin, staring seriously before him. It's like talking to Pan, he thought, and he went on hurriedly "Of course the whole of this Thames Valley area is very important from the point of view of Saxon migrations. It's almost certain that a great part of the inhabitants of Wessex came from the East and crossed the river near here at Dorchester".

"But that is most interesting" said Sven. "Do you really think so?" asked Elizabeth and then turning away contemptuously she added "I don't believe you know anything about it".

"That is true" said the boy "but your father makes the story so alive".

"If you're really interested we might go to the edge of the wood and see the hill from a closer vantage point", suggested Edwin.

Sven was on his feet immediately "I should like that so much" he exclaimed.

"Are you coming, Richard?" asked his father, but Richard was deep in a first reading of *The Possessed* and merely shook his head.

Mr. Newman bounded lightly across the treetrunks that lay in the path, his sandals thumping against his heels.

"Of course when I say that Saxons and British dwelt side by side, I don't deny that there *were* cases of horrible violence" they could hear him saying, and Sven's answering voice replying "But violence, I think, is often so beautiful".

O

"How happy Edwin seems" said Mrs. Rackham to her daughter "That boy's quite right, he *has* got the spirit of 'continual youth' as he called it".

Monica made no answer "I'm going down to the stream again" she said.

"I've never seen him look so young and gay" went on Mrs. Rackham.

"How funny" said her daughter, as she walked away "I was just thinking how absurd he looked, like a scout-master or something."

If I was one of those Virginia Woolf mothers, thought Mrs. Rackham, I should have been told what all this means long ago. It's much better as it is, however, she decided. Fond as I am of Monica, I wouldn't be able to help, whatever may be wrong. She has no power of resignation, no ability to seek refuge, she insists on fighting, on living even when life is unpleasant. Edwin, too, has that same total absorption in the affair of the moment. They want to wring every drop out of life. She smiled as she thought how they must despise her for living so much in books. A secondhand life they would probably call it. I prefer to have my people pre-digested, she decided, its easier, yes and wiser. To-day's undercurrents, for instance, how wearying! . . . and life was so short. She turned to her book, then laughed out loud as it came to her how little even she profited from her reading. Let me remember Miss Woodhouse's folly in interfering in the affairs of others she said, and began her twenty-third reading of *Emma*.

Monica took the lime green coat she was carrying over her arm and placed it on a large white stone by the edge of the stream. Then she sat down and rippled her fingers through the water. Every now and again she dabbed her forehead or smoothed her eyelids with her wet fingers. The afternoon had become intensely hot, there seemed to be no breath of air anywhere. Overhead, mosquitoes and midges hummed so that she was forced to pluck some wild mint from the stream to attempt to drive them away. The mint grew so shallowly that the whole plant came away suddenly as she touched it, and mud from the roots splashed over her white dress. Everything seemed discordant to her—the yellow green of her coat against the emerald grass, the crimson ribbons of the large straw hat which lay at her side against a clump of pink campion. Suddenly she saw a creature slithering up the trunk of an old tree, a creature brown-grey like the tree itself—it was a tree-creeper, but for a moment the little bird seemed to her like a rat. The rusty bullocks further up the stream stamped and swished their tails as they tried to drive the horseflies from their dung-caked flanks. There were always creatures like that who lived upon dirt, who nosed it out and unearthed it, however deeply it was hidden, however long, yes, even though all trace of it seemed vanished for twenty years, she thought. A shallow, vain, egocentric creature like that, with those untrustworthy, mocking cat's eyes. Twenty years ago, when they were first married and Edwin had told her, she had been so anxious to help. There had been incidents, it was true, but they had been so unimportant and they had become closer through fighting them together. But now after twenty years she felt she could do nothing; her pride was too hurt. All this fortnight, since the holiday began, she had been telling herself it could not be true and yet she knew she was not mistaken, to-day especially she felt sure of it. What could have altered things to make it possible? she reflected. It was true that she had been a bit uncertain in her feelings herself this year, but Edwin had understood so well that it was change of life that was coming to her early. Change of life had such strange results, that must be it—she seized on the idea eagerly—it was all fancy. How horrible that anything purely physical could make one believe such things and how cruel to Edwin that she had indulged them. How cruelly she had behaved, even if it was true, and somehow she felt again that it was. She had withdrawn her sympathy at the very moment Edwin needed it most: it was easy enough to realize that with one's mind, she thought, but the emotional revulsion was so great after twenty years' forgetfulness that she might only overcome it when events had moved beyond her reach. Whatever happens, she thought, I shall be so much to blame; and to Elizabeth who came running towards her along the bank of the stream she said aloud,

"If anything should go wrong, darling, in our lives, always remember I am to blame. I hadn't the courage to do as I should".

The moment she had said it she could have bitten her tongue out. The child was already too inclined to histrionics in this new phase of schoolgirl religious enthusiasm through which she was passing. Monica's fears were quite justified, Elizabeth rose at once to the situation, though she had no idea of the meaning of her mother's words.

"Brave Mummie" she said, putting her hand on Monica's arm.

Monica spoke almost harshly "No, darling, *not* brave Mummie. Self-dramatizing Mummie, if you like, Mummie who's got the heroine's part quite pat at rehearsals and in the wings, but who always fluffs her words when it comes to the night. Anything you like, my dear, but not *brave* Mummie".

Mummie's so strange and sarcastic sometimes, thought Elizabeth, anyone but me might think she was bitter, but I know her better. I know how brave and true and kind she is. I understand Daddy too, how much he needs my love. Richard never thinks about anything but his old books, so I have to help both of them. It's a kind of secret I have with myself—and God, she thought quickly. God loves and knows them all, even Grannie though she laughs at him. It's true what Miss Anstruther says— life's ever so exciting for anyone who's found Him; always something new and worthwhile to do, not just silly messing around with boys like Penelope Black and all those drips. That's what Sven wants, a lot of silly girls swooning about over him, like soppy Sinatra. That's what he would like from me, for all he keeps on saying I'm only a kid, but there's no time for waste of time Miss Anstruther says. I wish Sven hadn't come here, it's all been beastly since he did. It's ever since he came that Mummy's been snappy and Daddy keeps on showing off, not that it's for Sven, he wouldn't want to show off for a little pipsqueak like him. I oughtn't to talk like that about him, I must learn to love him. Love everyone, pray for them and set a good example that's all we can do. I can help all of them even Sven if I show how Christ wants us to live. People don't say so, but they're watching us Christians all the time, Miss Anstruther says. Ye are the salt of the Earth. A City that is set on a hill cannot be hid.

Monica's voice suddenly broke into her daughter's thoughts.

"Look, darling! On that larch tree there. See? A jay". There, indeed very close at hand sat a jay preening its rose feathers, its pastel shades harmonizing delicately with the soft green caterpillars of the larch. Suddenly it rose, with a flash of blue-green wing feathers, and flew off, screaming harshly. Immediately all the birds in the wood seemed to break into chattering. A cold wind blew across the stream. Monica shivered and drew her coat round her shoulders. "I think there's a storm coming up, darling" she said "Let's go back to Grannie".

"I think there's a storm coming up, but I'm glad we came all the same" said Edwin, as, somewhat out of breath, he reached the crest of the hills. "We've gone much farther than I ever intended, but the time's passed so quickly in talking. I'm afraid the others may get rather anxious, but still I think one has a right to enjoy oneself in one's own way sometimes, don't you?" Then not waiting for answer he continued "The Saxon settlement must have run right across the chain to the left here. Down below, you see, is Milkford, the outskirts run right up to the foot of the hills. It's quite an important town still, a sort of watering place, but it was even more important in medieval times. Of course there's nothing earlier, really, than thirteenth century" he said apologetically "but the castle's quite interesting—fifteenth century, you know, when the fortress is turning into the country house. We might run down and look at it later, would you like that?" he asked.

"That would be most nice" said Sven "but for some minutes I should like to rest here, please. The heat renders me most tired" and indeed beads of sweat were trickling down his brown chest where the line of his shirt lay open almost to his stomach.

Edwin turned away "Yes, you lie there a bit while I explore round the place" but he did not move far off. Suddenly Sven broke the silence.

"That is so lovely, your signet-ring. I should much like one of the same kind" he said.

"Would you?" said Edwin. "We must see what we can do about it".

Sven did not answer. It was nice to lie here in the sun and to feel that one was being watched, admired. It was boring staying with these Newmans. Richard, with his books had been bad enough at home, but there it did not matter, if he did not choose to come out swimming or skiing with the girls, he could be left behind. But here there were no girls, no sports, only books and talking and talking. He had hoped to watch the English girls bathing and to go dancing with them; they were said to be prudish, but all the same he was usually very irresistible. They would have run their hands through his hair like Karen, who looked so pretty when her own hair blew across her face and she smiled with those white teeth through the salt spray; or they would have stroked his fine brown legs as Sigrid when she buried them in sand and he brought his face close to her firm white breasts showing through her costume; or perhaps even an English girl more bold than the others would lie naked and soft under him on the sand like little Lili who had licked the salt sweat from his chest when he had done his part with her—different girls, but all of them, all of them wanting him as he had a right to be wanted, so handsome he felt that sometimes he almost wanted himself. But here there were no girls only books and talking. He had hoped much of Richard's sister, but she was only a child of sixteen and even so she was taken up with some rubbish about religion. With Mrs. Newman, too, he had thought he might have so much fun, after all she was not so old as Mrs. Thomas, the American woman, who had taken him out to cabarets and dances and given him presents last year when he was only seventeen. It had been most pleasant and he had learned from her so much that was useful. But this bitch treated him as though he was a child, it made him so glad that now he could hurt her. Even if Richard had made him his hero like Ekki Blomquist who followed him around with admiring eyes, little Ekki whom he liked to protect and pet and tease—but Richard thought only of his books. No, it was only Mr. Newman who had been kind to him and who admired him. He looked so gay and fine for forty-seven, he would be very pleased if he could look so at that age. But all the same it was very disturbing, it would not be pleasant if so kind a man should behave stupidly, it would be necessary to be very polite and very firm. For a little while still it would be nice to continue to be admired, also he would like to have the present of the ring, also he would like to make that bitch unhappy. Not that he liked to be naughty but it was not pleasant when one was not admired. What strange little white shells there were on the ground, like little Lili's ears, or his own curls when they fell from the nape of his neck at the barber's shop.

The same little crustacea lay all around Edwin, pressed into the soft ground by the tightly winding mesh of mossgrass. Little balls of rabbit droppings were scattered here and there. The hillside was carpet smooth but for an occasional red and yellow vetch that rose above the even level. Edwin peered closely at the turf, but he noticed nothing for his thoughts were far away.

If only I could collect my ideas, thought Edwin, but the blood pounds so at my temples. If only I could piece together how it had all led up to this. I think I have been feeling shut in by them all for a long time now, at any rate all this year. Richard with his books and Elizabeth with this priggish religious talk, and lately even Monica has seemed to be so sure of her values, so determinedly living in a world of beauty. All the best that's written, only the actions God approves, only the most beautiful in nature and art—it almost sickens me at times. It all seems to come out in their lack of charity to Sven. I wanted so to be kind to him, to show him that he was wanted, to make up for their priggish lack of courtesy. I understood what they meant when they said he was materialistic, animal, superficial, vain—but in some degree I felt that I was too and I wanted them to realize that. The children will always be afraid of physical pleasure in sex, afraid of their own bodies' lusts, afraid of the lusts of others for them. It's worse, somehow, when Mrs. Rackham's here because I can see the stunted shy, self-satisfied life they're heading for. But Monica is different, all the years she has understood my feelings about it, and at times has shared in them gloriously, but recently she's changed, "trying to put sex in its perspective" she would call it, but that's only another name for avoiding it because it's distasteful. It's true she's given me this physical reason but she said it so eagerly that it seemed like an excuse for doing what she's wanted to do for years. And now this has happened. What I thought to be kindness and sympathy for a rebel has re-awakened the old feeling of twenty years ago, the old sensual pattern of Gilbert and Heinrich and Bernard and the others, only more violently as it seems, and the blood is pulsing in my head as it used to then, only more loudly.

Suddenly he heard himself saying in a clear, artificial voice "I'm so glad that we should have become such good friends, Sven, and I hope you are too. I don't expect you realize what a very lonely man I am in some ways. Oh! I know how lucky I am in my family, but they're terribly narrow. I felt perhaps that you were feeling that too.

Richard, for example" by now Edwin was talking at break neck speed "he lives in books, takes no pleasure in the life around him. Now you must find that very strange, being so strong and lithe and well-made. Yes I'm afraid the truth of the matter is that my family are all what we call in England kill-joys, that is they get no real fun out of life. That's what I've so admired about you, you obviously get so *much* fun out of life. I think it's probably because I've allowed my wife to dominate the family so. You'll think it funny of me to say so, but I'm not really very much of a woman's man. I think women are inclined rather to be kill-joys. Do *you* think so?"

"Do I?" said Sven "do I think that women kill joy? No, oh no. Certainly not that" and he began to shake with laughter, but seeing Edwin's face twisted with combined excitement and alarm he controlled his amusement and added "but I think I so well understand what you may mean, you must tell me about this. But not here, I think, for it is now getting so dark and a rain spot has fallen on my face so that I think there will be a storm. Shall you not tell me in the town down there?"

"Of course!" said Edwin eagerly and he began to clamber down the hill. "We'll go into Milkford and I'll ring up from there to say we've been caught by the storm. If we can't get a car we may have to stay the night there. You won't mind that, will you? It'll give us a real chance to get to know each other, and they say the Bull's really a very decent old pub".

At first there had only been a few heavy drops of rain falling through the trees in the wood. Richard, who had reached the death of Stefan Trofimovich, positively refused to move, and even Mrs. Rackham who was being once more horrified and entranced by the vulgarity of Mrs. Elton preferred to take no notice. Then quite suddenly the storm had burst over their heads—the picnic things all shook under the blast of the thunder-clap and the whole wood was lit up by a great fork of lightning which seemed to strike obliquely at the nearby stream. Before a second and more deafening thunder clap had sounded, Mrs. Rackham had jumped to her feet.

"Come on, Richard, pack up the picnic basket. We mustn't stay under these trees with this lightning about. Make for the car and the clearing. Help me with the rugs, Elizabeth. Monica," she called "don't stand there, my dear, we'll all get drenched soon if we don't move, apart from the danger of the lightning".

But Monica stood a little away from them, her face chalk-white and her eyes round with terror. As the next fork of lightning zigzagged viciously in front of them she began to scream.

"Edwin, Edwin! My God! where are you? Oh pray God nothing happens. We must find him, we must find him" and she turned and ran down the little path. She had hardly gone a few paces when she tripped on a tree root and fell on her face, bruising her cheek and cutting the side of her chin.

Richard made as though to move towards her and then blushing scarlet, turned in the direction of the car. But already Elizabeth had run to her mother and, throwing herself on her she sobbed.

"Mummie, darling, Mummie darling, let's go away from this place".

"For heaven's sake, Monica", said Mrs. Rackham "pull yourself together. You're scaring the child out of her wits." She took her daughter's arm and started to pull her to her feet, but Monica pulled her arm away roughly

"We must find him" she said and began to weep bitterly.

"Stop this at once" said Mrs. Rackham sternly "Edwin's perfectly capable of looking after himself" and she led her sobbing daughter to the car. By now the rain was pouring down. Monica's fashionable hair style was washed across on to her face and strands of hair got stuck to the cut on her chin, meanwhile the blood ran down on to the white dress beneath. As they came to the clearing there was a blinding flash of lightning, followed by a crash. In a few moments smoke was ascending from the other side of the stream—one of the larches had been struck.

"*You* must drive, Richard" said Mrs. Rackham "Your mother's not at all well" and she helped her daughter into the back, as she did so she heard her mumbling "Oh God! don't let it happen! Oh God! don't let it happen!" That any daughter of mine should be superstitious over a storm, she thought.

"It's lucky, there's only the four of us this time" said Richard, as he started the car.

Elizabeth kicked his leg "You silly, thoughtless idiot, don't let Mummie hear you" she said.

I've failed again, thought Richard. When I was reading about Stefan Trofimovich's death, I wanted to be there so that I could make him happy, to tell him that for all his faults I knew he was a good man. But when my own mother is in trouble I can't say anything. It all sounds alright in books, but when I see people's faces—all that redness, wetness and ugliness and the noises they make—I feel ashamed for them and then I'm speechless and that makes me angry and I say cruel things. It was just like that when Sven was unhappy over that girl, I wanted to be his friend as Alyosha was to Kolya, to tell him that I knew he was often bad, but that I didn't mind but it was no good because I couldn't show my sympathy. I shall always live like this, cut off, although I think I understand more clearly than others. But how can I speak to Mother of her fears about Sven and that they are absurd? No I must always be shut in like this.

Nevertheless when they arrived home, he took his mother's arm "Don't worry, darling, nothing could happen I'm sure" he whispered. But Monica did not hear him, she was listening to the maid.

"Mr. Newman phoned, ma'am, to say that he and Mr. Sodeblom are stranded at Milkford and will be staying the night".

Monica walked straight into the drawing-room and sat, with set face, upon the sofa. "I am very tired, my dears, I'll have my dinner in my room. Mother would you be very kind and see Agnes in the kitchen, I don't want to be worried".

Richard and Elizabeth began to speak at once, as Mrs. Rackham went from the room.

"Can I get you some books, Mother?"

"Shall I help you to undress, Mummie?"

But such offers were premature, for at that moment a car sounded in the drive outside and a few minutes later Edwin rushed breathlessly into the room.

"Oh! you're here before us" he exclaimed "So you got my message. As the storm cleared, I thought it wasn't necessary to stay the night".

Sven had come into the room very quietly behind Edwin and now his voice sounded, speaking very slowly.

"Mr. Newman was so kind, he was so anxious that I should stay and see Milkford. But I thought you would be alarmed at our absence, Mrs. Newman. See, however, he has bought me this lovely ring, the stone has so strange a name—garnet. But he has not forgotten you, Mrs. Newman" and as Edwin motioned him to be silent, he went on "But, no, Mr. Newman, you must show your wife the gift or she will be upset that you gave me so lovely a ring and nothing for her. Look, it is a beautiful sapphire pendant, is it not a lovely stone? I chose it for you myself, I have a great taste for jewels".

Monica got to her feet "It is a pity" she said "that you speak such ghastly English. You say unfortunate things that a boy of your age cannot understand" and she walked from the room.

A few moments later Mrs. Rackham returned. "Look" said Sven "at the lovely pendant the kind Mr. Newman has bought for Mrs. Newman."

"Oh! but Edwin how sweet of you! It's charming looking" said his mother-in-law.

"But Mrs. Newman does not at all seem to like it" said Sven.

"Oh! she will to-morrow" said Mrs. Rackham "she's very overtired to-night, the storm upset her a lot".

The rainfall ceased after dinner and there was a calming silence as Monica sat before her dressing table, talking to her mother. Suddenly Edwin came into the room. He began to talk quickly as though he feared interruption.

"I've been talking to the children" he said "and Sven thinks he ought to return home by the next boat—that is in three days—I think he's right probably. He's got his exams coming on and I don't know that it's been quite his sort of holiday or" and he laughed "that we're exactly his sort of family".

Monica said nothing, but Mrs. Rackham declared approvingly "I'm sure it's a very wise decision".

"I'm glad you think so" he said "because I was wondering if you'd mind looking after the three of them until he goes. I've suddenly remembered *Don Giovanni* comes off next week and it may not be done again for some time". He put his hand on his wife's shoulder. "Would you like to go up to the flat for two nights on our own?" he asked.

Monica nodded her head "Yes, darling" she said "I would".

"You'll have to wear that new pendant to celebrate" said Mrs. Rackham.

"No" said Monica "I shan't do that. I don't think I shall ever wear that pendant. And now" she said, gathering her dressing-gown around her "I must go and see that all Sven's clothes are properly mended. I can't have Mrs. Sodeblom thinking we didn't look after the child, she was so good to Richard" and she swept from the room.

Safe, thought Edwin, safe, thank God! But the room seemed without air, almost stifling. He threw open one of the windows and let in a refreshing breeze that blew across from the hills.

THE END